# WITCHES AT WAR

# The Wickedest Witch

MARTIN HOWARD

ILLUSTRATIONS BY COLIN STIMPSON

WITCHES AT WAR I: The Wickedest Witch

Text by Martin Howard
Illustrations by Colin Stimpson

This edition published in 2009 by
Pavilion Children's Books
10 Southcombe Street
London
W14 0RA

An imprint of Anova Books Company Ltd

ISBN 9781843651314

A CIP catalogue record for this book is available
from the British Library.

10 9 8 7 6 5 4 3 2 1

Printed and bound by SNP Leefung Printers Ltd, China

This book can be ordered direct from the publisher
at the website: www.anovabooks.com,
or try your local bookshop.

# WITCHES AT WAR

## The Wickedest Witch

MARTIN HOWARD

ILLUSTRATIONS BY
COLIN STIMPSON

PAVILION
CHILDREN'S

# Contents

# Prologue

A small light glowed in a dormitory that was otherwise as black as a witch's knickers. From halfway down the row of beds came an exasperated whisper: "Drat!" A jumble of baggage had managed to burst – for the third time – out of a spotted red handkerchief tied to a stick. If you are going to run away to seek your destiny properly then you *must* have all your belongings tied up in a spotted red handkerchief on a stick and Sam always tried to do things properly. She just couldn't understand how to get three pairs of black jeans, a black dress, a selection of black t-shirts, two black pullovers, several changes of underwear (all black) and what was nearly a library's worth of books about magic into a handkerchief.

Sam loved reading books and had a particular weakness for tales about witches and wizards. She had waited patiently to be transported away to a land of magic (as generally happened in her books)...and waited...and then waited some more. Now she had decided that if the magic wouldn't come to *her* she would go to *it*. Luckily, she knew just where to start looking.

Waving a torch over the hopeless mess on her bed, Sam relented and pulled a battered pink rucksack out of a drawer. It was not quite the look she had been aiming for, but she was starting to think that people who ran away with only the clothes they could carry in a handkerchief probably got very smelly very quickly anyway.

She squashed everything in and pulled it onto her back. For the sake of tradition she then pushed some rolled-up socks into the handkerchief and hoisted the stick over her shoulder. Bending down, she picked up her most prized possession – a cone of flimsy black cardboard – and jammed it down on her head, before tip-toeing between two rows of beds where girls of all ages snuffled and snored. Climbing out of the dormitory window Sam took one last look around. Finally, she was leaving the orphanage behind. On her hat, stars cut out of silver paper twinkled in the moonlight. Sam grinned. She was running away to learn magic.

Across town was Pigsnout Wood. Everyone knew that a witch lived in the middle of Pigsnout Wood. And all witches need an apprentice.

# 1 Bye Bye Biddy

No one ever walks their dog in Pigsnout Wood for fear of never seeing Fido again. Things lurk in the shadows and occasionally jump out on unattended golden retrievers in a whirl of fangs and claws. It's the kind of tangled, gnarly wood where twigs grab at your hair and brambles try to eat your legs. Odd-smelling toadstools grow everywhere. The trees are covered in rope-like creepers and have weird, monstrous faces. They sound as if they are whispering nasty things about you, even when no breeze stirs their branches. It is a dark, haunted sort of place where there are ancient statues covered in ivy. For years there have been rumours and gossip about a witch living right in the middle and – for once – rumours and gossip are true.

It was the end of summer. The leaves were falling from the trees and the crescent moon was golden. In the middle of Pigsnout Wood was a crooked cottage, difficult to see in the moonlight because trees grew right up to the cracked and lumpy walls. Inside the cottage an old lady sat in a rocking chair by the fire and unfolded the newspaper. After a few moments she began to cackle horribly.

Esmelia Sniff, a witch, sat back in her chair smiling the kind of smile she smiled when something horrible had happened to someone else. Then she read the front page of *The Cackler* (the witches' newspaper – 'all the news wot is fit to line the cat's litter tray with') for a second time.

Emblazoned across the front page was a photograph of a witch so old that spiders had built cobwebs over her. At first glance she looked like a normal hag: the warts, pointy hat, black clothes and drool were all present and correct, but then you noticed that she had a safety pin through her nose and zips all over the place. This was a punk rock witch and her name was Old Biddy Vicious. She was also the Most Superior High and Wicked Witch, the owner of the Black Wand of Ohh Please Don't Turn Me Into Aaaaarghhh…Ribbett and the most powerful sorceress in all the world. Well, that is to say she *had* been.

Underneath the photo, *The Cackler*'s headline read:

## POISONED TO DEATH!

In general Esmelia liked people being dead (except herself, of course) as they were less annoying that way and didn't wriggle about so much on the plate. However, finding out another witch had popped her clogs was even better and guaranteed to make Esmelia's day. It confirmed her belief that all other witches were a bunch of lightweight, flibbertigibbets with no staying power. Even old Biddy had only made it to 148. It was shameful, a witch of her standing dying so young – and being murdered was no excuse. The world of witchcraft needed some shaking up and Esmelia knew just the person to do it. Eagerly, she flicked through the newspaper. There were pages and pages of kerfuffle about Old Biddy's death and what a great witch she had been, but Esmelia didn't bother reading any further. In her opinion any witch that allowed herself to get poisoned had it coming and certainly didn't deserve an eight page commemorative pull-out section. No, she was looking for something else. She found it near the bottom of page two and her eyes sparkled with an evil glint as she read:

> *Of course, now Old Biddy has been done in by some unknown assassin we'll have to get a new Most Superior High and Wicked Witch. Trials will start in one month's time in the grounds of the Bleak Fortress. Any witch what wishes to enter must have three signatures from other witches along with a few words saying why [Name of Applicant] would make a great Most Superior High and Wicked Witch…"*

Folding the paper with a snap, Esmelia looked over to her cat and said "Tiddles, pack up your fleas, we're moving on."

Tiddles looked up and yawned.

"Yes, my dear," Esmelia continued. "We will shortly be taking up residence in the Bleak Fortress of the Most Superior High and Wicked Witch. You'll like Transylvania, there's lots of...umm...weremice and suchlike. You'll love it there."

The one thing Esmelia wanted more than anything was to become Most Superior High and Wicked Witch. It wasn't just the idea of living in style at the Bleak Fortress or having the awesome power of the Black Wand of Ohh Please Don't Turn Me Into Aaaaarghhh...Ribbett at her fingertips. No, what Esmelia longed for was the chance to boss other witches around. If she was Most Superior High and Wicked Witch there would be no more of the modern witchcraft you got nowadays. All witches would be forced to wear black, familiars would be a traditional toad or black cat and midnight cackling over cauldrons would be put back on the curriculum.

Once she was in the contest Esmelia was sure she could win it – even if it did mean breaking the legs of her competiton – but there was one small problem: Where would she find three witches to recommend her?

Esmelia was not a popular witch. It was quite right and proper for a witch to hate another witch, but Esmelia didn't just detest her fellow hags, she looked down her nose at them, making it quite clear that they didn't reach the Esmelia Sniff standards of bad, old-fashioned witchery. Also, every now and again she would poke them in the eye. Very few people – not even witches – like being poked in the eye. In fact, everyone thought she was a crusty, miserable, smelly old baggage and tried to avoid her. And while Esmelia was quite proud of this, it did mean it would be tricky finding three witches who were prepared to sign up for having her as Most Superior High and Wicked Witch.

"Drat!" she exclaimed. 'Great big lumps of dog doings with flies buzzing round."

Swearing solved nothing. A different tactic was called for. One that would have immediate results. If Esmelia could magic up her own witches, it would be easy to hit them over the head with the poker until they agreed to recommend her. It had been a while since she had done any actual magic, but the old witch thought she remembered how it went. Snatching up the poker from the fire and pointing her finger at Tiddles, Esmelia chanted:

La la la and tiddly pum
Something about the power of one
I summon whatever rhymes with 'itch'
To turn this cat into a witch!

A bolt of magic was supposed to blast out of
Esmelia's finger. Tiddles should have disappeared, to be
replaced – in a puff of smoke and some glittery twinkles
– with a witch. Instead, a couple of sad-looking glints
dropped off Esmelia's finger as if it were a damp
firework. Tiddles yawned and went back to sleep.

Having tried the spell on an unsuspecting spider,
an ant crossing the stone floor and the pile of crusting
plates next to the sink, Esmelia admitted defeat. Her
specialties as a witch had, for a long time, been cursing,
cackling and rubbing her hands together. It had been a
long time since she practiced any real magic.

Pacing the floor, she tried to think of a solution her
her problem. She considered forging some signatures,
but becoming the Most Superior High and Wicked
Witch was a big deal and the judges were bound to
check. Finally, Esmelia wondered if she could get three
witches to recommend her by asking them nicely,
perhaps even going so far as to say "please." The thought
made her cackle so hard that her baggy old grey knickers

fell down around her ankles.

The only course of action left was to have a temper tantrum, so the old witch picked up a toad and prepared to throw it at the wall. "Aaarghh, blinkin', flippin', peskilential botheration!" she yelled.

There was a knock at the door. No one had knocked on Esmelia's door for many years.

Esmelia dropped the toad, who thanked whatever it is toads thank when they have a close shave with being splatted against the wall and slunk off under the dresser.

The hag scowled. Whoever was disturbing her toad tossing was in for a very bad time indeed.

# 2 The Apprentice

The front door creaked open with a deep creak, like a very old man bending over. Candlelight spilled from the cottage into the dark forest and the witch peered along the narrow path winding through the trees. There was nothing there. Cursing, she was about to slam the door when an annoyed voice spoke up: "I'm down here!"

Esmelia looked down to find a small and serious person frowning back up at her. A face that looked as though it had been attacked by every bramble and thorny branch in Pigsnout Wood. The face of a small girl. It was about waist height and had green eyes framed by long dark hair full of broken twigs. Perched on top of it was a dented pointy hat made from black cardboard and in the middle of the face was a nose that screwed itself up as Esmelia watched.

"Ugh, you smell," the girl said. "Do all witches smell? Will I have to smell?"

Esmelia ignored the questions, her rage forgotten. Instead, she began rubbing her bony hands together in glee.

"Hello, errrm…dearie," she said, attempting a

welcoming smile. It wasn't easy for her and she ended up looking like a spider had crawled into her mouth. She gave it another go, grinning so wide that the girl could see her teeth (of which there were two). Feeling that she had at last got it right, Esmelia continued, "Are you a poor little lamb what has lost its way in the dark forest?"

"No. What's wrong with your face?" The little girl asked.

Esmelia wasn't listening. She was already walking round and round the girl, still rubbing her hands together and with a little bit of dribble leaking out of the corner of her mouth. Very quietly, she was mumbling things like "Oooo yumyumyumyum," and "Yes, that's a nice leg, it'll go lovely in a stew, that leg. And look, there's another leg right next to it, what a stroke of luck." After a couple of minutes of this, during which the little girl folded her arms and looked sulky, Esmelia straightened up.

"Let's get you in the warm and dry shall we, you'll catch your death of cold out here in the rain."

"But it's quite a warm night and it's not even raining…"

"It's very changeable. You never know when it might start," said Esmelia briskly, bustling the girl into her kitchen. "Best to get you out of those wet things and into a nice warm pot."

The door creaked shut behind them. Esmelia sat her guest down in front of the fire and started piling logs into the stove. Tiddles wandered over and allowed Sam to scratch him behind the ears, then thanked her by sinking his claws into her leg. She pushed him away with her foot, looked around the cottage with interest and said, "It smells in here too."

"Yes, lovely isn't it?" Esmelia replied absently, throwing on more wood and using bellows to get the fire hotter. Without waiting for a reply, she continued. "Do your mammy and daddy know where you are?"

"My parents left me on the steps of the orphanage when I was a baby. I've run away."

"That's nice. I didn't have none neither. My mammy had me in a ditch and left me in the mud."

"But someone must have found you. Did you live in an orphanage too?"

"No dearie, I was raised by chickens." Esmelia picked up her best casserole dish and looked at Sam as if judging whether she would fit or not, which – of course – is exactly what she *was* doing.

"I've heard of people being raised by wolves or gorillas, but never by chickens," Sam said, tearing her gaze away from a toad under the dresser that had a finger to its lips and was shaking its head.

"Mmmm…the times we had squawking and pecking about in the dirt." Esmelia was now scrabbling through cupboards and piling up ingredients: salt, pepper, a little olive oil, a pinch of rosemary. "I'm not saying it's a patch on wolves, but if it's beady eyes you want, you can't have a better teacher than a hen."

Sam inspected Esmelia from across the room. She did have very beady eyes. "What happened?" she asked.

"Well, it ain't easy pecking when you've got no beak and I got hungrier and hungrier and them chickens started to look plumper and tenderer."

"They raised you from a baby and you *ate* them?"

"Oh yes and very tasty they was too. A lovely crispy skin if I recall." Esmelia stalked across the room, pinched Sam on the arm and cackled. "Not much meat on you, but I reckon in about half an hour you're going to be nice and crispy too, dearie."

This was the point at which little girls were supposed to start screaming and running for the door, only to find it locked. The old witch had been looking forward to it.

Instead Sam re-crossed her arms and scowled. "Please stop calling me 'dearie,' my name is Sam. And you can't eat *me*."

"Why ever not dearie?" Esmelia replied in surprise.

"Let's see, you're a skinny but tasty-looking little girl alone in the woods at night and I'm a witch. Some people would say 'wicked' witch, but I prefer to think of myself as just a traditional crone trying to stick to the old ways in a world gone mad. Any way you look at it, it seems to me I'd be failing in my duty if I didn't eat you."

"Yes, but I'm your apprentice."

"My what?"

"Your apprentice, you know… like a trainee. You're going to teach me all your mystic secrets and magic spells. Potions, broomstick flying…" Sam glared at Esmelia. "I'm your apprentice," she repeated firmly.

"No you're not, you're my supper." Despite herself, Esmelia was taken aback. This was not supposed to happen. Where was the screaming and the fighting? She *liked* the screaming and the fighting.

"Besides," said Sam. "I bought sandwiches."

"Made out of eyeballs?" Esmelia asked hopefully.

Her new assistant looked up sternly. "No, they're cheese and coleslaw. I don't eat meat…or bits of face either."

This was all going horribly wrong, but Esmelia wasn't to be beaten so easily. "Look dearie, you've obviously made an effort with the hat and everything, but I really am starving hungry and I don't need an apprentice witch…"

Just then a little maggot of an idea crawled into Esmelia's head. An apprentice witch. A *witch*. A witch could recommend her as Most Superior High and Wicked Witch, couldn't she? A witch could even help her win. And meanwhile, she could be fattening the little scrag up for a celebration feast.

Esmelia stroked her hairy chin. Eventually she spoke. "Well…Got any black clothes?"

"Oh yes. Lots." Sam nodded enthusiastically.

"Hmmm…any woodcutters likely to come looking for you?"

"Any what?"

"Beefy men. Big axes…Not fussy about whose head they cut off."

"Oh no, I don't know anyone like that."

Esmelia stroked her chin for a while longer. "Alright," she said eventually. "You can sleep in the attic. I take breakfast at three in the afternoon sharp and if you give me any cheek it'll be headfirst into the oven for you, alright?"

Sam nodded so hard her head nearly fell off. She asked, "Can I start learning magic now?"

Esmelia showed off her two teeth again. "Yes dearie. The magic of washing up and the magic of cleaning out the cat's litter tray. Now you get on with it or you'll be learning the magic of a wallop round the back of the head."

# 3 Rats in the Attic

As Sam cleaned the dirtiest pans she had ever seen and helped the toad escape while Esmelia wasn't looking, the old witch fired up her cauldron. An evil plot was called for and that meant cackling over a cauldron. When it was bubbling nicely, Esmelia checked the old grandfather clock to make sure it was midnight and began to stir the sludge within, mumbling about dark deeds by moonlight and the state of her feet.

Sam looked on curiously and asked, "What are you doing? Is it magic?"

Esmelia scowled at the interruption. "Ain't you never seen a witch plotting evil, err... plots before?"

Sam shook her head, ignoring Esmelia's glare. "Is that a magic potion?" she asked.

Esmelia flapped her hands to shut Sam up. She wasn't about to admit it, but she had avoided making magic potions since her last disaster. It was supposed to make her grow a few new warts but had left her skin smooth and radiant, while reducing the fine lines of ageing. The pot actually contained a snail stew she'd made earlier for dinner, but it was more than good enough for plotting with: a wicked witch could plot over a boiling kettle if she mumbled and cackled enough. Staring into the bubbling mess Esmelia saw a snail trying to do backstroke and at last a plan began to form...

Every witch she'd ever met hated her, it was true, but there were bound to be one or two who hadn't heard of Esmelia Sniff, weren't there? Witches living miles away from anywhere who might be daft enough to recommend her as Most Superior High and Wicked Witch. All she had to do was find two and once the girl had her passed her witch's test she could sign the third. How difficult could that be?

With the satisfaction of a plot well-hatched, Esmelia ladled some of the stew into a bowl and sat at the table. Sam buttered some bread for her own supper and tried to look out of the window as much as possible. The crunching, squelching noises coming from the other side of the table were bad enough, but the sight of the witch's two yellow teeth munching the grey mess made Sam feel ill, particularly when one plucky snail made a break for freedom down her chin and was sucked back in again. Finally, after she had washed up the slimy snail pan, Sam was led upstairs.

Everything in the attic was covered with a thick layer of dust and cobwebs. Creaky beams supported the straw roof and the floor was bare wooden boards. A shaft of moonlight poured through a small window made from diamond-shaped panes of glass. At one end a brass bed looked as if its mattress had been used as a trampoline by a troupe of elephants and the whole room was crammed with junk – moth-eaten rugs, an old-fashioned tin bath, broomsticks with only a couple of twigs left, wooden chests, various broken bits of furniture and a variety of stuffed animals.

For a girl who had spent her life sleeping alongside nineteen other girls in a neat orphanage dormitory that always smelled of disinfectant it was heaven. "It's amazing," Sam said, picking up a skull with a dribbly candle on top and blowing away the dust.

Esmelia looked round at the piles of junk, wondering if she had missed something. "Well it ain't the Ritz Hotel, but when I was a girl learning the witching under Old Nanna Wonk I had to sleep on top of the wardrobe," she said.

"Oh," Sam replied politely. "Why did you do that?"

"The rats ate me bed," said Esmelia. "Nasty little

beggars. I got my own back though… look they're over there in the corner."

Sam looked over to where Esmelia was pointing to a family of stuffed rats on top of a chest of drawers. All of them were on their knees with little ratty paws clasped in front as if pleading for mercy.

Leaving Sam to settle in, Esmelia went off to do some research. This involved leafing through a copy of *Which Witch?* and marking the witches who lived a long way away and didn't get out much. Meanwhile, her new apprentice unpacked the pink rucksack. Then she spent several hours shifting, sweeping, tidying and putting some of the more disturbing stuffed animals in chests where they couldn't stare at her. By the time the sky outside started to lighten, the attic room looked like a proper bedroom for an apprentice witch. As the last of the night's bats swooped away, Sam changed into her black pyjamas and climbed into the bed – which squeaked and buckled under her weight exactly as she had hoped it would – and blew out the candle on top of the skull. It had been a long night, but she already felt more at home in the witch's attic than she ever had at the orphanage. Within seconds she was snoring.

Many miles away, the murderer of Old Biddy Vicious dropped a velvet cover over her crystal ball. So, she thought to herself, Esmelia Sniff was planning to enter to competition to become Most Superior High and Wickedest Witch, was she? Perfect.

The murderer picked up a fluffy white kitten called Mr Popsy and stroked it. "Mandy," she said in a voice that was smooth and warm and lovely. "You *must* make sure Esmelia finds her way to me. She will make an excellent Most Superior High and Wicked Witch, don't you think?"

Another witch stepped out of the shadow. This one had dyed blonde hair as well as clothes that were several sizes too small and many years too young for her.

"What, Stinky Sniff?" she snorted. "She's an absolute twonk. You can't be serious. Besides, I thought *you* were going to be Most Superior High and Wicked Witch, your delectable majesticness."

"Dear Mandy," the murderer yawned. "You're really very stupid as well as being old and ugly. Let me explain. The most powerful witches in all the world will enter the Most Superior High and Wicked Witch trials. It would be a chore even for me to kill them all. And boring too. Plus, what would it *look* like, do you think? Me, a power-crazed evil sorceress, entering a competition like any *ordinary* witch? It would be embarrassing. No, it will be much better to have some dimwit do all the hard work. We'll make sure that she's the last witch standing, then, just as she's about to be crowned... Ooops, I've bumped her off and grabbed the Black Wand of Ohh Please Don't Turn Me Into Aaaaarghhh...Ribbett for myself. Everyone hates Esmelia anyway, so there won't be any fuss."

Mandy Snoutley clapped her hands in excitement. "Ooo," she cried. "Diabolica Nightshade, you are simply the worst, the most evil, the wickedest witch *ever!*"

"I know," Diabolica – also known as "Deadly" – Nightshade replied with a small smile of pride. She smoothed her long, dark hair, leant over and pulled a tasselled rope. Deep below in the dungeons, a bell rang. "And I've made sure I can control everything once the trials start. Now, where's Igor? I think a glass of champagne is in order, don't you?"

# 4 How To Make a Hag

Next afternoon, after breakfast, Esmelia leaned back in her chair and blew on the cup of steaming hot drink she called "tea" but which smelled like it had been made from something scraped off the toilet floor. She looked Sam up and down. "Now then…" she said. "Errr… what was your name?"

"Sam," replied Sam obediently.

"Sam?" Esmelia paused. "That ain't a witch's name. It ain't even a girl's name. It should be Miseretta or Snaggletoothed Jane or something like that."

"It's short for Samantha which I don't like because it sounds like someone sneezing."

"Humph, well it'll have to do. Right then, I've sent away for your witch licence and your test'll be in three weeks."

"Witch licence?" The apprentice asked excitedly.

"Until you've passed the test it's only provisional, but you're allowed to practice basic witchcraft and when you're a full witch you can do stuff like, ooo I don't know… maybe recommend someone for Most Superior High and Wicked Witch."

"So what do I have to do to pass this test?"

"Cast a simple spell, make a potion, show that you can ride a broomstick, curse a bit and register your familiar." Esmelia walked over to a bookshelf and started making a pile of books on the table. Sam was pleased to see that some of them were large and leather-bound, definitely the sort of book that contained mystic-knowledge-beyond-the-ken-of-man, though hopefully not beyond-the-ken-of-Sam.

"That's *The Skyway Code*, you'll be tested on that." Esmelia said, dropping the book on the table with a thud. "And this is *The Witchionary*, you'll need it for your spelling. *Potions for Pillocks*, of course and *How to Curse Friends and Influence People*, that goes without saying. Plonking it on the table with the rest, she turned back to the shelf and pulled out a ragged looking volume. "And here's...oh, this is a book of handsome wizards in their underpants," she muttered. "I don't know how that got in there." She stuffed the book back onto the shelf hurriedly.

The mound of books was large and growing quickly. Sam stared at it then at the crone looming above her. "I've got to learn all this in three weeks?"

"Three weeks," Esmelia replied flatly. "If you don't pass, you're fired. And when I say fired, I mean boiled, roasted and drizzled in gravy."

Sam reached out for the top book and snatched her hand away. She looked up at Esmelia questioningly. "They don't bite or scream or make demons come pouring out of the pages to eat my head, do they?"

The old witch spoke as if she were talking to an idiot. "They're books. Books. Paper and ink and a bit of glue. Not generally known for eating heads is your books. You've seen a book before, haven't you?"

"Yes, but these are *magic* books."

"I don't know what they teach youngsters these days… They're books. No book never did no one any harm."

Stretching out a hand again, Sam opened *How to Curse Friends and Influence People.* At once a screeching voice began hurling insults at her and the air turned blue. Sam's hair blew back and her paper hat flew off.

"Except that one," said Esmelia. "You have to be a bit careful with that one." She closed the book and slammed it on the table a couple of times yelling, "Shut up in there!" then opened it again. All was quiet. "There, now let's have a look at you."

Sam stood by the kitchen table and Esmelia walked around her. "Black clothes, that's good, though a raggedy old dress and shawl beats jeans every time. No warts, that's bad. Long hair, bit on the greasy side, so that's alright, but you might want to put some more twigs and insects in there. Too many teeth. I could knock some out if you wanted?" Esmelia curled her hand into a fist and made a punching gesture.

The apprentice shook her head.

"No?" asked the witch, "Well don't say I didn't offer."

She paced around her apprentice again. "Now, give me look at that hat."

Picking up the paper cone, Sam pushed out a new dent and handed it to Esmelia, who peered at it closely, humming and haaing as she prodded it and twisted it this way and that. Then she screwed it into a ball and tossed it on the fire. Sam screamed and leapt toward the grate, reaching for her beloved hat, but it was already ablaze. Esmelia grabbed her by the back of her sweater.

"Whoever heard of a witch in a paper hat?" she whispered into Sam's ear.

"But it's the only one I've got," Sam began to sniffle.

Esmelia continued. "If you don't scare the living wotsits out of people you ain't got no right to call yourself a witch. You've got to be *nasty*. And no one's going to be frightened of a paper hat. You might as well wear one of them bow ties that spins around and a set of plastic fangs."

Sam struggled towards the burning paper.

"But you can't *not* have a hat, so you'll have to borrow my spare."

Sam stopped struggling and looked up.

Esmelia opened a cupboard and lifted out a hat. It

was tattered and torn. There were holes in it. The top sagged over to one side and the brim was floppy. But it was pointy, black, made of proper material and had an unmistakable air of witchiness about it.

Sam stared at it in wonder.

Esmelia carried the hat across the room and carefully set it on her apprentice's head. "There," she said with satisfaction. She paused, then continued, "It suits you actually. Not everyone can wear hats, but on you it looks good."

Beneath a hat so large that only the bottom of her chin could be seen Sam nodded. The movement made the brim come loose and it fell to her shoulders, making Sam look as though she'd put her head through a paper hoop.

"Yes, it's definitely you," Esmelia said twisting her face into what she hoped was a smile of encouragement. It looked like she was chewing a wasp. Not that Sam could see from beneath the hat.

"Anyway, mustn't stand here chatting all day," the witch said, rubbing her hands together. "Work to be done. Off you go."

Sam took a couple of steps towards the washing up, tripped on a chair and fell in a sprawl.

"Perhaps if we cut a couple of eye holes," Esmelia muttered.

# 5 Being Nasty

That night Sam sat in bed with a pair of scissors, a needle and black cotton and Esmelia's second-best hat resting on her knees. By candlelight she snipped and sewed and when the sewing didn't demand her full attention she glanced across at a book that was propped up against a stuffed badger. It was smelly and dusty (the book not the badger, though that was smelly and dusty too) and filled with spidery writing. In fact, the kind of book that Sam had learned to read for. It was called *Think Yourself Witch: 101 Steps Towards Becoming a Crone*, by Lilith

Dwale. If you had asked her, Sam would not have been able to tell you why she had chosen this particular book from the pile, it had just seemed like the right thing to do. While her needle dipped in and out, Sam squinted in the golden glow of candlelight and read…

*So, you have three weeks to become a witch.*

She blinked. How did the book know she only had three weeks? Perhaps all apprentice witches were given three weeks she thought and read on.

*Most witches study for years to pass their test, but something tells me you'll be a natural Sam.*

"Oh," Sam said, quickly followed by "ow" when she pricked her finger with the needle in surprise.

*And you can take that look off your face; it's magic, stupid. What were you expecting?*

"Well, I thought it would be waving wands and sparkles and stuff like that," Sam admitted, feeling a bit silly for talking to a book.

The writing on the page twisted and changed.

*We'll get to that soon enough, but let's see what you've learned so far shall we? Being a witch is all about how you think. Take this easy quiz to find out if you've got what it takes.*

Sam looked. The quiz consisted of just one question:

*The witch you are apprenticed to plots to use you in her plans to become Most Superior High and Wicked Witch and then cook you in the oven. Do you...*

*a. Skip around the place singing "fa la la la la" all the livelong day. You're sure it will all turn out alright.*

*b. Help her with her plans and hope that she grows to like you so much that she won't want to eat you.*

*c. Wait until the best possible moment then turn the tables on her and become Most Superior High and Wicked Witch yourself.*

Sam thought carefully. Then thought some more. She was tempted to tick *b*. Esmelia was clearly mad as goats and quite horrid with it, but she had been kind in her own funny way. Well, kind for someone who was planning to eat her. She *had* lent Sam her second best hat and *was* helping her become a witch. On the other hand Most Superior High and Wicked Witch did sound like a fun thing to be...

Finally, Sam marked *c.*, saying out loud, "but I don't want to upset Esmelia too much."

As she watched the letters in *Think Yourself Witch* dissolved and reformed. Now the page read…

> *Mostly C's: Is the right answer, but remember you'll never get to be Most Superior High and Wicked Witch unless you think like a witch. That means you'll have to be diabolically nasty so you may as well learn to enjoy it.*

Sam nodded uncertainly. Aside from calling a teacher a 'twit' once when she'd had her book taken away during geography, she had never been nasty. By way of practice she scowled at the stuffed badger for no reason whatsoever, then shut *Think Yourself Witch* and took up her sewing again. As the candle dribbled onto the skull, she held up the hat and looked at it critically. It was patched and mended and still looked a bit lopsided, but there were no holes and the brim was now firmly attached. Best of all it fit her head perfectly. Placing it gently on the bedside table, by the pile of books, Sam read the titles on the spines again. Nervously, she reached out to a heavy book entitled *Spells*. After all, she only had three weeks.

# 6 Broom With a View

The next day Sam propped *Spells* open on her side of the table and hid behind it. She had learned very quickly not to talk to Esmelia before or during breakfast. She had tried it once and had to duck out of the way as the witch's finger poked at her eye. Some people are not very good for an hour or two after they've woken up and Esmelia was one of them, though, to be fair, she wasn't particularly friendly whatever the time of day. Instead, Sam memorized an incantation for making an object vanish from one place and appear somewhere else. One of the book's previous owners had noted in pencil at the bottom, "good for theevin fings." Lost in the instructions, Sam munched mushrooms and sipped water until she heard Esmelia push her plate away and fill her cup from the cracked china pot.

Peering out from behind the book cautiously and ready to dodge back at the first sign of a gnarled finger jabbing across the table, Sam coughed to attract attention.

"Got a frog in your throat?" the old witch asked nastily.

"No," said Sam.

"Would you like one?" Esmelia reached into a pocket and pulled out a struggling frog. "I was saving it for later, but you'll never get nice and, umm…tall… if you don't eat a decent breakfast."

"Thank you, but no," the apprentice answered as politely as she could and tried not to wince while Esmelia harrumphed and shoved the poor kicking creature back into a pocket. "I was just wondering what you could tell me about the Most Superior High and Wicked Witch."

Esmelia's eyes turned beadier than a bag of beads. "What do you want to know about that for?" she hissed.

"Just something I read. I was curious," Sam answered, looking into the witch's glare. "And you mentioned it yesterday."

Esmelia harrumphed again. For a minute everything was still apart from a lump in Esmelia's pocket that hopped up and down until the old witch swatted it. Sam frowned as the little frog gently keeled over under the heavy black material. Then, the witch stood slowly and took an old-fashioned black cloak from a peg on the wall and swirled it around her shoulders. She held it out so it looked like a huge pair of bat wings and loomed over Sam. It seemed like the cottage suddenly became much darker. And then Esmelia began to cackle.

It started with a drawn-out "Nyarrrrrrrrrghhh," accompanied by eye rolling, then became a hacking "ahuhuhuhuhuhu" like an old engine coughing into life. This got louder until it was an ear-piercing "he he hee HEE, ARGGHAHA HAHA!"

As a glass on the dresser shattered. Esmelia's cackle drew to a close with a chest-rattling "Meeeheheurrgh" as a final flourish. "*I* am the Most Superior High and Wicked Witch," she screeched. "Waver of the Black Wand of Ohh Please Don't Turn Me Into Aaaaarghhh…Ribbett and the most powerful witch in all the world."

"Are you really?" Sam asked, impressed.

There was an embarrassed pause. Esmelia's arms fell to her sides. "Well, no. Not in actual fact. Not what you might call *officially*. Not yet at any rate. But I soon will be. And in the meantime, you and I are going a-visiting."

Sam's eyes widened. A chance to meet more witches? And to travel? Aside from a couple of dull museum trips, Esmelia's cottage was the furthest from the orphanage she'd ever been. Grinning, she looked up and asked, "Where are we going?"

Esmelia flapped her hand, "Oh, around and about. Which means you'll have to learn how to ride a broom."

"But, w…what about my test?" Sam spluttered.

"We'll be home in time for that and you can learn on the way."

For Sam it was as if all her dreams had come true.

A few hours later, she wasn't so sure. From below Esmelia's voice called out, "That's it. You're getting it now. A little more the other way up though."

Upside down and level with the tops of the trees Sam wrapped her legs tighter round the broomstick and squeezed her eyes shut. On the bright side, she thought to herself, her hat had stayed on really well. There was no mistaking that she was a witch. On the other hand, you didn't see many witches clutching onto their brooms from underneath as they were thrown about the evening sky.

Down on the ground Esmelia looked up at the girl hanging from a broom. "Now, just pull the handle gently towards the ground..." she shouted up. "That's right and... ooooo, you didn't want to do that."

In front of her the broom was stuck in the ground with its twiggy end in the air, quivering. As Esmelia watched happily, Sam slid down the handle into a crumpled heap on the grass.

The old witch bent over and picked up Sam's hat, which was now pancake-shaped. After brushing it down and pulling the point out into a cone again, she peered closely at it. "Here, that's some lovely needlework you done on that," she said.

"Thank you," came the muffled reply from the heap on the ground.

"Up you get then. No time for laying around all night."

Painfully, Sam pulled herself to her feet. Grunting with effort, she pulled the broom out of the ground and swung her leg over it, just as Esmelia gave a tiny whistle.

The broom took off vertically, like a rocket, trailing a small girl behind. A drawn out "waaaaaaaah," faded in Esmelia's ears as Sam disappeared into the heavens. The crone's bony shoulders heaved with cruel laughter. Above, the black dot that was Sam zipped around in crazy zig-zags against the moon. Esmelia could just about make out faint squeals. Still chuckling, she strolled back to the cottage. There was plenty of time for a snooze while the cheeky little beggar got on with the serious business of learning.

# 7 One Enchanted Evening

After dinner, a stiff and bruised Sam sat at the kitchen table with her book and glanced over to the fire where Esmelia was in her usual place, her hat pulled down over her eyes. Judging from the snores and the gurgles and the drooling the old witch was fast asleep. Briefly, Sam wondered whether she ought to wait for Esmelia to show her how to do magic, but already knew she couldn't. She had been waiting her whole life and now here it was right in front of her. She already knew the spell by heart and Lilith Dwale had said she looked like a natural. She was sure she could do it.

Under her breath Sam muttered the words on the yellowing page.

Instantly, a curious feeling like a swarm of tiny bees whipped around her body. It felt as if her hair was standing on end, like her body had been filled up with a fizzy drink and shaken. Like she was bursting with power.

Magic.

*Real* magic. Filling her up and making her blood sparkle. It felt like she could do *anything*.

## THE WICKEDEST WITCH

With eyes as big as dinner plates, Sam made a mystic sign in Esmelia's direction with her fingers, just as it showed in the step-by-step diagrams. She sent her magic out, curling invisible around the snoring witch. She was sure she could move Esmelia to the moon with a flick of her fingers and a single command. But no, her first spell would be cast to try and save a life. Just a little one. That poor frog had been in the old witch's pocket all day. Sam hoped it was alright.

She moved her fingers again and felt the magic snag something. A white sparkle appeared above the table briefly then disappeared, leaving behind a small frog. Sam reached out and picked it up. After a day of being knocked around and swatted, it was quite, quite dead. A tear pricked the corner of Sam's eye and she scowled in Esmelia's direction, then sneaked out of the cottage and into the forest where she dug a hole. She slipped the frog into it with a few words, then covered it softly with earth and a little pile of stones.

Behind her in the cottage, one of Esmelia's eyelids twitched and she tutted softly to herself. Really, she thought, the girl had *some* talent, you had to give her that. Not many could pull any magic off on their first ever go and fewer still without blowing their own ears off. Even so, the crone told herself, she's not proper *witch*

material. Not the right sort to be a real witch at all. She was nowhere near nasty enough.

Many miles away, Diabolica Nightshade looked into her crystal ball. Hmm, she thought to herself, the girl was quite powerful. Not that it made any difference to her plans, she was just a little girl after all. Nevertheless, Sam was quite, what was the word? Ah yes… interesting.

She shook her beautiful thick head of hair. It wouldn't do to get sidetracked. "Mandy," she said. "I think it's time to go to press."

"Yes, your divine munchiness," replied Mandy, "*The Cackler* is yours to command."

"Good, let's start by making sure that no one else recommends the old bag for Most Superior High and Wicked Witch. I want her to be desperate by the time she finds me."

# 8 Licensed to Spell

Esmelia tore open two packages that had been left on the doorstep that morning by a terrified postman who never manged to deliver to the cottage in the woods wihout returning with ripped trousers and a head full of woodlice. The first envelope contained Sam's Provisional Witching Licence and a letter confirming the date of her test.Esmelia threw both on the table and eagerly unfolded *The Cackler*, which had arrived in the second envelope. This was news she'd been waiting for.

'ALL THE LATEST ON THE TRIALS!' the headline screamed. Esmelia's eyes darted backwards and forwards as she read the smaller writing underneath:

> *Mandy Snoutly,* The Cackler's *gorgeous young ace reporter, writes that preparation for the Most Superior High and Wicked Witch trials are fully under way. The judging panel of Most Superior Witch contestants will be:*
>
> *Tiffany Toadlick, Leader of the Grand Coven.*
>
> *Scary Doris, Legendary ten-time winner of*

*the Warts and All Prize.*

*And, for the first time, the panel will also include a wizard, Dr Sulfurus Cowl. A Grand Coven spokeswitch explained that Dr Sulfurus had been invited because "Tiffany fancies him and wants to snog him, euurgh."*

*Although no contestants have yet confirmed,* The Cackler *can exclusively reveal that among those witches looking for recommendations are Mad Elaine de la Moustache of France and Transylvania's vampire-witch the Dark Mistress Cakula von Drakula. There are also rumours that Esmelia Sniff is planning to enter the race. Mandy Snoutley reminds all witches that Esmelia smells of dirty toilets and has less brains than a monkey's bum. If she comes poking around looking for a recommendation do not, under any circumstances, open the door to her.*

Esmelia snorted in disgust. How dare they? She'd as much right as anyone. Well, she'd show them; those other witches didn't stand a chance. She had met Mad Elaine de la Moustache and she was just a bad tempered old bint who babbled away in some funny language all the time. Cakula von Drakula, on the other hand, was a completely different kettle of disgusting black goo. She was not just a witch, but a vampire too and would be difficult to beat in a fair competition. Luckily, Esmelia had never played fair in her life and was not about to start now.

"What's that you're reading?" asked a yawning Sam from the foot of the stairs.

"Never you mind," replied the old witch grumpily, folding the paper up quickly and shoving it in a pocket. "Just something telling people about the Most Superior High and Wicked Witch competition. That's all. Nothing else."

Sam popped a slice of bread under the grill of Esmelia's wonky old oven. "Oh," she said. "Where's it going to be?"

"Transylvania," snapped the crone.

The apprentice began spreading green jam that she suspected was made from stinging nettles, on her toast. She had been surprised by how nice it was. "Cool," she said, "I've never been abroad before. When do we have to be there?"

"Trials start the day after your test. Oh and your licence came."

There was a crash as Sam's plate smashed on the floor.

"Now look what you've done! All over the floor,

too," Esmelia screeched. "That mashed caterpillar jam doesn't just make itself you know."

Snatching up her witches' licence Sam twittered. "It's here… Look I'm witch number BMH81680085BUM! … The BMH stands for Black and Midnight Hag and the BUM! is just to be rude…"

She was stopped abruptly by a broomful of bristles jabbed in her stomach. An unbreakfasted Esmelia was in no mood for this much talk.

"Out!" she shrieked as she pushed her apprentice through the door. "Get out. Do some broom practice. We leave tomorrow."

As Sam sprawled in the drift of dead leaves Esmelia threw the broom out after her. "Wait!" the trainee cried, ducking and holding up her licence. "Does this mean I'm a proper witch now?"

"No," Esmelia scowled. "You ain't got a familiar yet. We'll sort *that* out at sunset." Then she slammed the door and rubbed her hands together briefly in satisfaction. Though she'd always had a natural talent for slamming doors, it did no harm to practice.

# 9 Vroom on the Broom

Tucking her new licence in her back pocket, Sam frowned and picked up the broom. Having spent an informative couple of hours in bed with *The Skyway Code* she was ready for it.

Before climbing on, she sat cross-legged with the broomstick across her knees and began talking to it. Axes were mentioned. So were fires. Sam explained how she might be forced, if it did not co-operate, to pull its twigs out one by one. As she spoke it began to tremble under her fingers and when she stood it floated alongside her, at a polite level to swing a leg over. So, Sam thought to herself, sometimes nastiness does pay.

With heels wedged into the twigs as the illustrations in *The Skyway Code* showed, she gripped the handle and lifted her eyes to the sky. Beneath her the ground dropped away. Unlike yesterday, though, the flight was smooth. Twitching her fingers to tell the broom to stop, Sam held her breath with excitement and spun slowly in the air, allowing the breeze to choose her direction. Then, leaning in close to the handle, she whispered two words: "Show me."

Instantly the stick leapt forward. Over forests, towns and fields she swept. The wind should have torn her from her stick. She should have frozen. But though the air roared in her ears and she felt slightly chillier than she had on the ground, it wasn't uncomfortable. *The Skyway Code* said that this was part of the spell cast on all broomsticks, a spell that is very long and difficult and a speciality of three witches who live in Germany. Looking down at the handle Sam noticed the small brass plaque with the initials of witches Bumsling, Moidor and Wibble. Esmelia's broom was the very best.

No chores got done that afternoon. Instead, Sam raced for miles through the air with a grin splitting her face. She was a witch. She had a licence, a hat and a book of spells. Tonight there would be a familiar... Ooops. Sam pulled the broom to a stop and glanced at the sinking sun. She had forgotten about the familiar and now had no idea where she was. For a moment she almost panicked. Then she reminded herself again that she was a witch. Touching the broom beneath her she whispered "home" and nearly fell off with relief as it swung around and swooped off in a new direction.

Ten minutes later she dropped to the ground by Esmelia's cottage. The sun was setting.

"Where've you been you skiving little toad?"

shouted a harsh voice. "You're supposed to be here apprenticing. I've had to trim me own wart hair and I *told* you we had stuff to do tonight."

Esmelia stepped out of the cottage door with a face like an angry parsnip, caught her grinning apprentice by the elbow and pulled her off into the forest.

# 10 Well Met By Moonlight

Esmelia was in a huff and it had little to do with Sam being away all afternoon. Usually she was in a huff for no particular reason except she liked to maintain a low-level huff at all times for appearances sake, but this evening was different. The huff was larger than usual and the reason for this humungous huff was that Esmelia would have to do proper magic and her feelings about that were very different to Sam's.

Once upon a time, she'd been good at it, but she'd used magic less and less as the years went by. She disliked that it was all a bit glittery and silly when you came right down to it and made her feel like she should be singing "bibbety bobbety boo" or something. Still, if the girl was going to pass her test it had to be done, plus of course it would do no harm to practice for the Most Superior High and Wicked Witch trials. She'd need to be in tip-top magical shape after all. Esmelia gritted her teeth as well as she could, there just being the two of them and led the way to a secret clearing in the woods. It was a difficult place for a witch to find. For a non-witch it would have been impossible.

"Why do we have to go into the woods?" Sam asked. The path was getting narrower and even though she was now a witch, Pigsnout Woods still gave her goosebumps. She could swear that the trees were leaning in on purpose to scratch her, though none of them touched Esmelia and there were eyes shining in the darkness that looked too far off the ground to belong to average woodland animals.

Esmelia ignored her and began the lesson on familiars. "For thousands of years witches and magical creatures have teamed up. The creature gets someone to look after it and the witch gets a...what's that word? It means someone that doesn't completely hate them."

"A friend," said Sam.

"Yes one of them sort of things, I expect," Esmelia replied, her face twisting in distaste. "But a *friend* who can be useful if you want to turn someone's head inside out with magic. A familiar, in fact."

"And that's what we're doing tonight, isn't it?" asked the trainee eagerly. "Finding my familiar?"

Esmelia ignored her again and stopped suddenly so that Sam walked into her back, then said quietly, "And this is why we've gone into the woods."

Before the two witches was a small clearing. By the light of the rising moon it was enchanting. Wild flowers grew everywhere and the trees surrounding it stood taller and straighter as if standing guard. In the centre was a ring of high stones with other stones laid across the top. Just like a circle of doorways Sam thought to herself, which is exactly what they were, in a very odd way.

"It's beautiful," she whispered.

"It's a right pain in the bum to find," Esmelia grumped. She briefly considered telling Sam that this was a place where you could travel between strange realms, but decided not to. Esmelia had snooped and sniffed through the books Sam had brought with her and guessed the girl would only get all happy about it and Esmelia couldn't stand to see her smiling little face. Instead she said, "It's a sort of meeting place."

"Who built it?"

Esmelia shrugged, "Don't know, don't care," she said. "Now go sit in the middle."

Obediently, Sam went to sit in the very centre of the stone circle. The air around her was gently sizzling with magic.

Meanwhile, Esmelia furrowed her brow with concentration and began to walk around the stones three times (she was supposed to dance, but Esmelia would rather have eaten her own legs than use them to dance, thankyouverymuch, so she just waggled her foot every few steps). As she went she chanted a spell so old that it was in Ancient Egyptian. Each part of it called out a summoning to a different part of the animal kingdom and translated something like this:

Here puss, puss, puss
Here kitty, kitty
Come on boy,
Here boy, good boy, *good* boy
Who's a pretty polly den
Pretty polly, pretty polly

And so on, until all the animals had been called, except fish – which always died before anyone could get them home and made awful familiars anyway.

When the spell was finished the air shimmered briefly with green light as the call went out to every corner of the globe. The clearing fell quiet. Esmelia thought about a quick cackle of triumph, but decided against it. You really needed thunder and lightening for a decent triumphant cackle. Instead, she strolled over to where Sam sat cross-legged. Regarding her trainee sternly, Esmelia said, "Right then. This is an ancient ritual and very dangerous, so you stay where you are until it's over. You're not to move at all, unless you need to stretch your legs a bit or go to the toilet behind a bush. Understood?"

Sam nodded.

"In a while your familiar will come to you. In the meantime you're to think about animals, but no cats; Tiddles will go spare if you bring another cat back. Try for a toad. You know what they say?"

Sam shook her head.

"A cat for a witch means nary a glitch
But a witch with a toad has a lighter load."

Sam looked up blankly. "I know," said Esmelia. "It's rubbish. Anyway, you sit here 'til it turns up and that's all there is to it."

Esmelia strolled away rummaging in her huge pockets for a mushed up newt sandwich and a flask of poison mushroom tea. Settling herself under a tree, she waited.

And waited.

And waited.

After about three hours the moon was high, but no animal had crept into the circle. The girl had not moved an inch, but now a tear sparkled down her cheek in the moonlight. Esmelia shrugged. Sometimes it didn't work out. But no familiar, no witch; the rules were clear. Oh well, it looked as though she might be getting a decent meal earlier than she had thought. It would mean finding an extra witch to sign her up and that would be a bother, but at least there would be enough of Sam to keep her well fed for a few days. In the meantime she was getting bored and there was something about that serious little face now crying openly that made Esmelia feel... She shook her head. She was just tired and, after all, it had been lots of fun tormenting the girl with the broom yesterday so she was feeling...Well, she didn't dislike the little maggot quite as much as normal. It didn't really matter as it looked like the pot for her anyway, but she'd give it one more hour and as she had nothing else to do, she might as well pass the time. Esmelia pulled a knife from a pocket and walked into the woods until she found a stick that was exactly right, then she sat back down under her tree and began whittling.

Two hours later the old witch walked over to her silently weeping apprentice.

"Never mind," she said. "It just means that not a single animal in the world wants to be your friend and you can't never be a witch."

The apprentice looked up. Before she could stop

herself, Esmelia found that she was holding out the stick that she had been whittling. Giving someone a gift was a new experience for her and she felt a strange, warm glow in her belly. Quickly, she reminded herself that Sam would soon be bubbling away in the oven and managed to squeak, "Made this. You can have it."

Sam reached up and took the wand. Esmelia had carved a handle and a design of ivy twisting round it. It was beautifully done. When you live in a cottage in the middle of the woods without television and only a lot of sharp knives for entertainment it's amazing what you become good at.

"Some witches like a wand," the old witch said. "There are many ways they can be used. Maybe I'll show you."

Sam's face crumpled. "But… but I can't be a witch without a fuh… fuh… fuhmiliar," she howled.

Just then there was a tiny rustle in the grass. Both witches looked down. Climbing onto Sam's foot was the biggest beetle either of them had ever seen. That is to say it was larger than most beetles, not that it was the size of a horse or anything like that. It had huge pincers, which it waved as if to say "hello."

Sam gasped and put her hand out to it. The beetle climbed on and looked up at Sam with – if such a thing is possible – a look of love on its little beetle face.

"What are you going to call him?" Esmelia asked, straightening up and starting off towards the forest path.

"Ringo," said Sam, while Ringo fell asleep on her shoulder. He had flown and walked a long, long way, which is why he was late.

"Funny name for a beetle," replied Esmelia.

"Hmmm," said the apprentice, then added thoughtfully, "But is it OK having a beetle familiar? I thought it was supposed to be a toad or a cat?"

Esmelia glanced over her shoulder at Sam. "Opinion is divided. I'm not saying I approve, but at least it's black. These days you get witches with all sorts of familiars what shouldn't be allowed. There's Kideeta Skingh in India. *She's* got an elephant called Nelhi. And

Macy Bloomingdale in New York, who's got a worm named Goliath. And that Swiss witch Heidi Gurdi has a dog without a nose."

"A dog without a nose? How does it smell?" Sam asked.

"Not bad, she gives it a bath once a week regular."

Far far away, Diabolica Nightshade watched Esmelia and Sam in her crystal ball. "Mandy," she called sweetly. "Time for stage two of the plan. Just pop over to England and give Esmelia a little hint about where to come, would you?"

"As you command, your succulentness," replied Mandy Snoutley picking up her broom.

# 11 Bad Press

Sam opened her eyes at dawn, wakened by the sound of little beetle feet running around on the bedside table. After a while it stopped and Ringo began bobbing up and down. Almost as if he's doing press-ups, she mused. In fact, the beetle was doing press-ups. He was very strict about his morning training. Sam leaned over to kiss his shiny black back then snuggled back under the covers to catch up on her sleep.

The thumping began ten seconds later. Esmelia was banging on the ceiling with the broom.

"Get a move on you lazy little slug," she crowed as Sam came down the stairs dragging her rucksack, "and get on the dratted broom."

There is a certain type of irritating person who cannot possibly go any sort of long journey without leaving at the crack of dawn. No one knows why. Esmelia was one of them. She never usually got up until well after everyone else had finished lunch but today the sun was just creeping over the horizon and the old witch was packed, breakfasted and tapping her foot impatiently.

Sulkily, the apprentice left the cottage with a hasty slice of bread hanging from her mouth while she checked that Ringo was safely in her breast pocket. Throwing the rucksack on her back she climbed on the broom near the twiggy end, which was already occupied by Tiddles. Finally, Esmelia took her place at the front. She blew her nose with a stinky old hanky and arranged herself in readiness for take off.

At that moment a flurry of dyed hair, perfume and heavy make-up dropped through the branches accompanied by the whirring click-click-click of a camera.

"Stunning young lovely Mandy Snoutley from *The Cackler*," boomed a loud voice as a witch with an enormous chest got off her broom. She was dressed as if she were going to a disco even though she looked about eighty-four and was snapping away at Sam and Esmelia. Sam could hear the witch's corset creak from ten feet away.

"Don't move," shouted Mandy Snoutley. "That's beautiful. Big smiles now."

Sam smiled automatically, the slice of bread falling from her mouth and even Esmelia's face screwed itself up into an unpleasant-looking new arrangement.

"Super, gorgeous, fabulous," cried Mandy Snoutley.

"So, Esmelia, you're off to find a bunch of idiots to recommend you as Most Superior High and Wicked Witch, are you?"

The attempted smile disappeared from Esmelia's face as quickly as it had arrived and her finger jabbed out at the journalist's eye.

Mandy dodged deftly and pulled a notebook and pencil from the band of her pointed hat.

"I'll just put 'yes' shall I?" she asked and scrawled that down without waiting for a reply. "Bootfaced old pig's bum Esmelia Sniff," she went on, "confirmed to *The Cackler*'s chief reporter, the slender and lovely Mandy Snoutley, that she would be combing the world for three witches daft enough to be fooled into recommending her for the top job."

"I never said no such thing. I'm going to visit a friend." Esmelia lied furiously.

"Esmelia Sniff" the journalist continued scribbling, "today said that there were bound to be three witches out there with less brains than a box of bellybutton fluff."

Meanwhile, Esmelia, whose face was now purple, was digging around in her bag. "Where's that old wand," she muttered. "I knows I put it in here."

"And what's this?" Mandy asked, pointing her pencil at Sam. "A light snack for the journey?"

"No. I'm Sam, her apprentice," said Sam cheerfully. "I've got a licence and everything."

"Shutupshutupshutup don't tell her anything," screeched Esmelia. "I *said* we're going shopping."

"Got your test soon by any chance, eh Sam? That'll be one down, then, eh Esmelia?" the journalist chortled. Mandy began scribbling in her notebook again. "Who knows readers, perhaps Stinky Sniff will find two more. So far only *Diabolica Nightshade* has said she would give Esmelia a recommendation, but is there anyone else out there mad enough? You can trust that your number one reporter, the luscious Mandy, will be the first to find out."

Esmelia, who had stopped listening, gave a yowl of triumph and pulled a wand from her bag. She twisted her head to look at Sam. "I told you I'd show you how to use one of these things, didn't I?"

Sam nodded.

"Oi! You know we're not allowed to use magic on each other," Mandy said sharply taking a step back.

"Allowed? *Allowed*? I ain't never given a thrupenny widdle for *allowed*," Esmelia replied hotly. The wand twitched and the broom shot forward. Sam gripped Esmelia's back as they swept into the sky. "Besides," continued Esmelia, "it weren't magic I had in mind."

Below them Mandy Snoutly lay on her back, tugging at a wand that was wedged firmly up her nose.

"There are many ways to use a wand," Esmelia shouted over the wind to Sam, "but *that* is my all-time favourite."

Diabolica Nightshade peered once more into her crystal ball. She had a terrible urge to cackle, but reminded herself that only the stupid, old-fashioned warts-and-no-teeth kind of witch, cackled. Instead she allowed herself a small giggle. The look on Mandy's face! Really, Esmelia might be the worst kind of cauldron-botherer, but you had to admire nastiness like that...

# 12 The Good Old Days

Thousands of feet above the unrolling countryside, Sam clung to Esmelia's bony back and asked, "Who was that?"

Esmelia had been hiding copies of *The Cackler* from Sam because a. she didn't want the girl knowing too much, b. they had written a lot of nasty things about her and c. it was hers and if the little toad wanted to read it, she could buy her own. Nevertheless, she had to tell the girl something or she'd be on and on at her all day. Really, Esmelia thought, she didn't know what young people today were coming to. Going around asking questions and being annoying. When she was an apprentice she had never annoyed Old Nanna Wonk. Well, she corrected herself, she had tried, but considering Nanna was spent almost all the time believing she was a cheese sandwich, she wasn't the sort to get annoyed easily.

Esmelia stared into the distance and let her mind wander back to the days when she'd been an apprentice herself. Old Nanna had been as nutty as a squirrel's breakfast. The cheese sandwich obsession hadn't been that bad really, but the whole thing about Nanna being dead every so often had been just plain odd. Esmelia had tried poking her with a stick, but the dead are very relaxed about poking. Eventually, she had given up and just kept Nanna slumped over in her chair as a kind of ornament.

"That person with the camera?" Sam persisted. Esmelia scowled. "Nobodythatyouneedtoworryaboutdearie," she mumbled in her best crone's mumble.

"Eh?" Sam replied cupping an ear. "You'll have to speak up a bit, it's windy."

Great Dog's Toilet! Esmelia exclaimed to herself. The little insect doesn't know when to shut up. Buzz, buzz, buzz at you all day. "She's a reporter from *The Cackler*, alright? Witches' newspaper," she yelled angrily. "All the news wot's fit to line the cat's litter tray with. Got that? Happy now?"

"There's a newspaper for witches?" Sam asked. "That's *so* cool. Do you have a copy?"

Drat it, Esmelia thought. If it stops her buzzing for half an hour… She dug around in her bag and handed Sam yesterday's *Cackler*.

Twenty seconds later, the apprentice sucked air between her teeth. "Sheesh, they don't like *you* at all, do they?" she shouted through the wind.

Snatching the paper back, Esmelia's voice turned even more nasty than usual. "It's disgusting what they print these days. Look at this: 'Elvirissa Pursley Ate My Hamster.' That's news is it? Well, I've met Elvirissa Pursley and she'd eat *anything* that isn't nailed down. It would be news if she *didn't* eat your hamster. And this," Esmelia continued, jabbing at another headline. " 'Aliens Turned My Cat Into a Stick of Rhubarb.' That's old Madge 'Rhubarb' Wigstippler. She turns everything into rhubarb and then blames aliens. Well known for it."

Esmelia scrunched the paper into a ball and tossed it out into the air. "It's all rubbish, " she said. "Aliens don't even *like* rhubarb. Aliens like…"

"It says that you wouldn't make a very good Most Superior High and Wicked Witch," Sam interrupted.

"They hates me because I've got me views about the craft," Esmelia shouted sniffily. "I remembers the days when all witches were dirty old crones in raggedy dresses. Covered in warts we was in those days and liked nothing better than turning anything that moved into frogs. Oh, we may have poisoned the odd apple and cursed a bit, but it was all in fun. And then people would rush around with flaming torches and pitchforks trying to burn you…" she sighed. "They was good times."

Esmelia stared sadly at a passing seagull, thinking of a time when people would scramble to get indoors if they saw her coming. These days they had lost their fear of witches. Last time she went to the village someone had tried to help her across the road and a woman from the old folks' home had pressed some leaflets into her hand and whispered something about rubber knickers. Esmelia had been so upset she almost forgot to steal the cheeky young whippersnapper's purse.

Sam, too, was thinking. Eventually, she asked, "So you're going to bring back the good old days when you're

Most Superior High and Wicked Witch?"

"Yep. With knobs on I reckon."

Sam frowned. The old days didn't sound that good at all. She had never liked wearing dresses, raggedy or otherwise and she didn't much fancy people trying to burn her either. Her idea of witchcraft, it seemed, was a lot different to Esmelia's and it would be horrible if just as she was starting to enjoy herself she had to go around being all bent up and gnarled and end up with flames licking at her feet. Anything licking your feet is fairly horrible, but flames, she thought, would be the absolute worst. After a while she carefully let go of Esmelia and fished around in her rucksack until she found *Think Yourself Witch* by Lilith Dwale. Making sure that Esmelia was still staring into space, daydreaming about the olden days, she opened the book and began to read…

*Don't forget, you'll need three recommendations from other witches to enter the Most Superior High and Wicked Witch trials and of course you mustn't tell Esmelia anything. She'd only try and eat you, plus you want her to find out at exactly the right moment. A nasty surprise like that shouldn't be wasted…*

Below, the Atlantic Ocean rolled on. It was big, grey and nowhere near as interesting as Sam's book.

# 13 Ghost Town

Sam awoke with a start. Having exhausted the in-flight entertainment, (which consisted of reading and picking a scab on her elbow), she had dozed off against Esmelia's back. Now they were over land again and the broom was descending towards a forest so big and so beautiful it made Pigsnout Wood look like a patch of stinging nettles. The colours of the autumn leaves took Sam's breath away. In fact, the two witches had reached New England, which is as famous now for its spectacular autumn colours as it once was for being the centre of the witching world. These days though, it just had the one witch and according to *Which Witch?* she wasn't strictly a proper witch. At least not by Esmelia's standards. But she had a licence and that was all that mattered. It meant she could recommend someone for Most Superior High and Wicked Witch.

The broom touched down in the middle of the forest. At first, Sam thought Esmelia must have made a mistake. There was nothing to see except neverending trees. Then she spotted an old sign. In peeling paint she read "Welcome to Sawyer Bottom: Population 2,976 0".

In the shadows beneath heavy branches were old, dark, abandoned houses. Roofs had fallen in and walls were in ruins. Moss grew over everything and even the air smelled rotten.

"Ghost town," Esmelia muttered.

"We learned about ghost towns at school," said Sam. "They're towns where everyone moved away and just left empty houses, aren't they?"

Esmelia gave Sam one of her bewildered looks and sneered, "Errr, no. They're towns where *ghosts* live. The clue's in the name you see: *Ghost* town. A town for *ghosts*. So-called because everyone's dead."

"But how can anyone *live* somewhere if they're *dead*?" Sam asked. "That's just stupid. Besides, there's no such thing as…" Sam saw a white, almost transparent shape drift past out of the corner of her eye and decided to shut up. She looked around nervously and shuffled a little closer to Esmelia. It was getting dark.

"We prefer the term 'bodily impaired' to 'dead'", came a voice from behind. "And there's nothing wrong with not having a body. It shouldn't mean you can't have a full and useful lif… err… existence. It just makes it a bit more difficult to play tennis." The two witches turned to see a rather portly woman walking through the trees towards them. She wore thick glasses and carried a large old-fashioned tape recorder as well as various cameras.

Sam watched Esmelia's face wrinkle in disgust. She could imagine what the old witch was thinking. There wasn't a pointy hat in sight, let alone decent, black clothes.

Esmelia stepped forward. "Blanche Nightly?" she asked as politely as she could manage, which is to say that she only curled her lip a very little bit and made sure her eyeball-poking finger was tucked in a pocket.

The new witch bowed slightly. "That's me: Blanche Nightly, Ghost Hunter."

Blanche leaned in towards Sam and Esmelia. "Don't suppose you've seen any have you?"

Sam pointed to where the transparent wraith was floating. At once Blanche shouted, "Amazing!" and became a flurry of activity. Cameras clicked and whirred and various buttons were pressed on the tape recorder. In a loud voice, as if she were talking to a deaf person, the ghost hunter said, "We mean you no harm, oh spirit. Please make yourself known. Can you hear me? Knock once for yes and twice for no. Do you have a message from beyond the grave?"

Sam watched as the ghost, who appeared to be a quite attractive young man if a bit see-through and wispy around the edges, twirled his finger at the side of his head, said, "You're a loony, you are," before vanishing into the gloom.

# 14 The Curious Shade of Lilith Dwale

"So Mistress Sniff, the spirits are saying that you want me to recommend you as Most Superior High and Wicked Witch, is that right?"

It was two hours later and Esmelia and Blanche were sat in the only house in Sawyer Bottom that wasn't crumbling to the ground. Warm yellow lights came from the fire and a single candle, which lit Blanche's face as she sat with eyes closed and hands stretched out on the table in front of her.

Esmelia was doing her best to be pleasant, but the strain was showing. Under the table Sam could see her jabbing a fork into her own leg. This was to stop herself jabbing it into Blanche's. She had already told the ghost hunter sixteen times that she was looking for a recommendation

"That's right Witch Nightly," Esmelia replied with a tiny cackle. "You just write a short letter explaining why you think I'm the best for the job." She paused and continued under her breath, "and I won't hit you with the poker... Or not until you've finished it at any rate."

Blanche held up a finger, "Before that the denizens of the world beyond the veil are asking about your *qualifications*, ma'am?"

"Qualifications?" Esmelia looked down at herself, puzzled. "Well, as you can see I am a witch. Is that a qualification, eh? Being a witch?"

"I mean your leadership skills, what training you have, that sort of thing…"

Esmelia dropped the fork. "Ooops! butterfingers," she snapped and ducked under the table to delve in her bag for the poker.

"And they also want to know why you've come all the way here rather than asking your neighbours."

Esmelia's head bobbed up above the table again. She'd met some fruit loops before, but this witch was so far round the bend you'd have to use binoculars to see her and she was bringing on a throbbing headache. Esmelia's face ached with trying to smile and she'd been *nice* for two hours, sixteen minutes and thirty-three seconds, which was two hours, sixteen minutes and thirty-three seconds more than her previous personal best. Well, *nice* wasn't doing any good, so now it was time for a change of plan.

Seeing Esmelia pulling the poker out of her bag beneath the table, Sam interrupted, "Esmelia is a very traditional witch who would like to bring back cursing people, eating children, plus big warty noses and chins."

Esmelia glared at her. "I never said nothing about big chins. Big chins is optional."

"I see," Blanche cut in. "Back to the old ways is it? People burning witches and all that silliness?"

Esmelia was finding it increasingly difficult not to leap across the table and grab the other witch by the throat. "Maybe," she said nastily. "And maybe we could start them off burning witches what pokes about with dead people."

"Is that a *threat* Mistress Sniff?"

"No, that was me saying what I might *maybe* do. A *threat* would be if I pulled a poker out of my bag like *this*, stood up like *so* and shouted 'WRITE THE BLINKIN' LETTER OR I'LL TURN YOUR HEAD INTO A RASPBERRY FLAN.' *That* would be a threat."

Blanche ignored Esmelia and closed her eyes again, swaying slightly. "Hmm," she said. "The spirits are saying you must be tired out after your long journey, so we should see about writing your recommendation in the morning."

Esmelia lowered the poker slightly. "We should?" she asked, surprised and slightly disappointed. She was in a bashing mood now.

When she was sure that Esmelia was fast asleep (she could tell because the old witch was snoring so hard that her bed was moving across the floor and one of the windows had smashed and fallen out), Sam crept down

wooden stairs on her bare feet. Blanche Nightly was still sitting at the table with her eyes closed. Sat across from her was a ghost: a slim woman with long hair and a bent old hat. She had her chin in her hands and was gazing at Sam with interest. Sam felt a little jolt of recognition. She knew this witch from somewhere. The phantasm gave Sam a cheeky wink and a grin then vanished. As Sam walked silently across the floor Blanche muttered, "On the shelf, by the fire."

Sam padded over and reached down a slip of paper. In the dying firelight she read:

*I Blanche Nightly, recommend for the post of Most Superior High and Wicked Witch a fine witch of whom we can expect great things. Witches and wizard of the judging panel I give you Esmelia Sniff's apprentice, the witch called Sam, on condition that she passes her test.*

Yours, etc.
Blanche Nightly
(Presenter of TV's *My Pants are Haunted*)

"How did you know?" Sam whispered.

Blanche Nightly opened her eyes. For a second she didn't seem quite such a harmless oddball any more. Her eyes looked as if they had seen things that people are not supposed to see. And there was something else there – a tiny glint of wickedness. Whatever Esmelia might think, Sam decided, Blanche *was* a proper witch. The ghost hunter's voice sounded firmer than it had earlier when she said, "I haven't spoken to Lilith Dwale in twenty years, but for the last few days her spirit hasn't left me alone. I owed her a favour, so I told her I'd recommend you if you seemed decent enough."

"Thanks," said Sam. "That was her, wasn't it?"

Blanche smiled mysteriously. "Oh yes. She wanted a look at you. Actually, she's been here all night. You should have heard some of the things she was saying about Esmelia Sniff. It was all I could do not to laugh."

# 15 Sam 1: Esmelia 0

"You low-down, fibbing, slimy, no-good heap of dog droppings!" Esmelia screeched. "You said you'd write it."

"I said I *might* write it," Blanche Nightly replied calmly. "And now I've decided to support another witch. I don't want to argue with you about it."

"No? Well you can argue with Mr Poker then," the old witch dived into her bag once more.

Esmelia straightened, holding the length of cold iron. She held it up and brought it crashing down towards Blanche, who didn't move. Before it could reach her, the poker twisted and bent out of the way. With a harrumph Esmelia tried again. Once more the metal twisted to miss Blanche, but this time it also flew out of Esmelia's hand and started flying around the room.

"Sorry," said Blanche Nightly. "It's the ghosts. They can be a bit naughty sometimes."

The poker was being joined by plates and cups and cutlery and the ornaments from Blanche's shelves. Everywhere she looked Sam could see things zipping through the air.

"Dead people don't frighten me," Esmelia snarled

loudly. "Silly beggars should learn to take a hint. Being dead is nature's way of telling them to get lost."

The ghost hunter looked outraged. "Don't say that!" she cried. "You'll upset them."

It was too late. A cup whirled out of the hurricane inside Blanche's house and smashed on the side of Esmelia's head. She screeched. It was followed by two saucers and a picture frame. There was the tinkle of broken glass and another shriek. Sam tugged at Esmelia's skirt. "Maybe we ought to get going," she shouted. "The broom's all ready."

87

"Thank you so much for dropping by," the Ghost Hunter smiled through the chaos. "It's been wonderful to meet you."

"Speak for yourself," snapped Esmelia. She turned on her heel crashed through the door, followed by a hail of crockery. Sam looked back to see the faint spectre of Lilith Dwale holding a plate and standing next to Blanche. The dead witch and the Ghost Hunter both waved farewell. Sam patted her chest making sure the letter of recommendation was safely tucked in her vest then followed after Esmelia.

Esmelia's huff was enormous. The two witches had been sat on the speeding broom for hours with not a word spoken, but Sam could feel the giant huff oozing from Esmelia's back. Reminding herself that she had her test in under less than three weeks the apprentice tried to ignore it and memorize a spell for making yourself invisible with Ringo reading from her shoulder. According to the book's former owner, this spell was "good for theevin' fings too." Sam shook her head sadly. Really, she thought, the world of witchcraft needed some shaking up. When she was Most Superior High and Wicked Witch she would introduce a Code of Conduct.

It would include not using magic to steal and definitely not plotting to eat your apprentice. She wondered briefly if Esmelia could be forced to wash occasionally before deciding that was probably asking too much.

In the meantime Invisibility was an easy spell and soon committed to memory. After a while she felt a tickling at her neck. Ringo learned quickly too. Sam flipped the page. And after a few moments flipped it again. She didn't know it, but she was learning magic faster than any witch in history. And Ringo wasn't doing too badly either.

# 16 Deadly Nightshade

A week later Esmelia's mood had not improved in the slightest. Thanks to what *The Cackler* had written about her, she hadn't found a single witch who was prepared to recommend her. The two of them had zig-zagged across the country and dropped in on three dozen witches. The American Indian witch called Ugly-Woman-Who-Picks-Nose told them that the Great Sky Bogie had ordered her never to use a pen. Mammy No-Legs chased them across fields in a wheelchair while waving a shotgun. The strangely named Miss Weekly Shopping had turned herself into a bowl of fruit to avoid talking to them. By now, Esmelia was completely fed up with sleeping in barns, usually with a load of stinking cows.

On the eighth day, Sam closed her book of spells and said, "What about that Diabolica Nightshade the reporter from *The Cackler* told you about?"

"Eh?" said Esmelia. Listening to other people was not one of her strong points, especially when they were getting right on her nerves, so she hadn't heard Mandy Snoutley mention Diabolica.

"You remember; she said no witch would sign you up apart from Diabolica Nightshade, who was a bit mad."

"Oh yes, her," Esmelia replied. Admitting she didn't know something was another of her not-very-strong points. They flew on into the whipping wind. After a while the old witch said, "Remind me where this Diabolica Nightshade lives. I seems to have momentarily forgotten."

"She didn't say."

"Right, right. Course she didn't," Esmelia harrumphed and started digging around in her bag for her copy of *Which Witch?*.

Two hours later they flew into a small thunderstorm that appeared out of nowhere. Esmelia brought the broomstick to a sudden stop and mumbled, "I smells a witch."

Below was a house on a craggy hill. It was an old and dirty mansion with turrets and the sort of dark windows that faces look out of. Ivy climbed the walls and there was a graveyard to the rear. It could not have looked more witchy if it was wearing a pointed hat and warty rubber nose.

A few moments later Sam found herself standing before a huge door, pulling on a rusty chain. Deep inside the mansion a bell clanged as if it were signalling the end of the world. Thunder rumbled and rain lashed at them. The door creaked open with a creak that sounded like a coffin lid swinging back. There, framed in the doorway, was… a girl; a few years older than Sam and with purple hair, but a similar impatient look on her face.

"Oh, it's you," she said flatly, as if the arrival of Sam and Esmelia was the most boring thing that had ever happened. In, like, her *whole* life.

Even Esmelia was taken aback. "You knew we was coming?"

"Yeah, mistress saw it in the great mystic thingummys. Parted the curtains of whatnot." The girl shrugged. "Or what*ever*."

She seemed to like shrugging, because she shrugged again. "Suppose you'd better come in. Mistress said so."

Lightening ripped the sky. The girl turned and led them past cobwebbed suits of armour and dribbly

candles until she pulled open a door and ushered them into a room of velvet and gold and warmth.

"Mistress," the girl said, as if she was talking to a bit of dog poo that was stuck to her shoe. "The, uh, weary travellers have arrived and that."

"Thank you Igor, that will be all," said a smooth voice.

Rolling her eyes, Igor left. The owner of the voice lay on a velvet sofa, before a great fire, wearing a tight black dress. Her dark hair billowed across velvet cushions and she looked up at her visitors with deep green eyes. Her ruby lips curled at the corners into a bewitching smile. Sam thought she'd never seen a woman so lovely, but there was something else about her, too. She was dangerous, Sam was certain. Still, she reminded herself, witches *all* seemed to be a bit dangerous. It was part of the job she supposed.

"Esmelia Sniff. I have been *longing* to meet you," the vision of beauty said. "Diabolica Nightshade at your service."

No one had ever been at Esmelia's service before. Her expression looked like she had just found a full-grown walrus in her sock drawer: a curious mixture of about 20 percent surprise, 50 percent indignation and 30 percent wariness.

"Please, take a seat Mistress Sniff," Diabolica continued. "I am *such* a great admirer of yours and will be delighted to recommend you for Most Superior High and Wicked Witch. But we have much to talk about first…" She patted a chair next to her. "Please sit, your apprentice can go with Igor to the dungeons."

Diabolica rang a bell by her side. "Igor," she shouted, as the girl reappeared, tutting. "Take this young lady downstairs with you, Mistress Sniff and I have important matters to discuss."

"How, like, *totally* interesting," replied Igor before muttering "*not*" while pushing Sam towards the door.

# 17 Dancing in the Dungeon

Igor walked stiffly down several sets of stairs lined with glittering candles and paintings (if Sam had looked more closely she would have realized that all of them were portraits of Diabolica). Everything about the older girl in front said "Do NOT try and talk to me." Finally they reached the dungeon. Looking around at the stone walls, grinning skeletons, chains and spiky metal things as well as the little bed, cheerful fire and the big poster of a pop star boy band, Sam shuddered and said, "Your mistress seems… err, very nice, Igor."

Igor whirled around, her face red. "My name is NOT Igor," she shouted. "It's Helza. Helza Poppin. *She* calls me Igor because *she* thinks every spooky old mansion should have a servant called Igor. She's not nice, she's *weird*."

Sam nodded and said, "Well, I'm Sam. And your mistress can't be as weird as Esmelia."

Helza pulled a face. "That's what you think. But does Esmelia bathe in donkey spit?"

Sam shook her head.

"Does she have a magic mirror that tells her she's a hot babe twenty times a day?"

Any mirror that was prepared to tell Esmelia she was a hot babe would have to be *really* magic, Sam thought. And blind, too. She shook her head again.

"Right and I bet she doesn't make you sleep in a dungeon for years when you should be out witching, either," Helza said angrily.

"You're a witch?" Sam asked, surprised. The girl wasn't wearing a pointy hat.

"Not just any old witch. I'm a *great* witch," Helza replied proudly. "There's no potion I can't make. I've even made up some new ones. I'd be famous if I could just get out of here."

"Then why don't you leave?"

Helza sneered down at Sam. "A witch's apprentice can't just *leave*," she said. "Don't you know *anything*? It's, like, *totally* against the rules. Only she can set you free. Her or the Most Superior High and Wicked Witch."

Sam raised a finger to her lips. "Ah," she said. "I might just be able to help you there."

"… so Mistress Sniff, the dark witch, Cakula von Drakula is planning to raise an army of witches to take over the whole world so she can drink everyone's blood. She must not be allowed to become Most Superior High and

Wicked Witch but only a witch as powerful and ingenious as the great Esmelia Sniff could hope to stop her..." Diabolica stopped her urgent whispering. "Mistress Sniff?"

Esmelia was peering at a cookie. After a long pause she asked, "are these bits of peanut and chocolate or bits of snot and rabbit poo?"

Diabolica looked puzzled. "Umm... peanut and chocolate I think. But, that is not important. Did you not hear me? The dark witch is rising!"

Esmelia slowly put the cookie back on the plate, pursing her lips with disapproval. Chocolate and peanut, she thought with a shudder; whatever next? Fixing her beady eyes on Diabolica, she said, "I heard you. Blah blah blah take over the world, blah blah blah drink everyone's blood."

"It must not be allowed!" gasped Diabolica.

"No? Witches will be witches, I always say."

"But she will be evil and cruel and..."

"...nasty?" finished Esmelia "A proper witch then? Good for her. Can't say I'd care so long as she don't try getting *me* in her army, but she *is* the competition I suppose. So what did you have in mind Mistress Nightshade? The garlic and the stake through the heart I suppose?"

"Well, yes. But mostly the stake."

"They're dangerous though, your vampire witches."

"Very," admitted Diabolica.

"So for the kind of witch who likes to stay in the shadows and meddle with people's lives, it would be much safer to have someone *else* do the pointy stick in the heart business."

"Much, much safer," Diabolica agreed.

"What kind of witch are *you*, Mistress Nightshade?"

Diabolica smiled. "Oh definitely the kind that likes to stay in the shadows and meddle with people's lives," she said. There was a pause while the two witches gazed at each other, then Diabolica threw a copy of *The Cackler* on the low table between them. "TWENTY REASONS TO HATE ESMELIA" the headline read. She followed it with *The American Cackler,* which had gone with "CRAZY BRIT WITCH ON THE LOOSE!" *The Australian Cackler*'s headline was "ESMELIA NOT WELCOME DOWN UNDER." Mandy had made absolutely sure that Esmelia wouldn't find her recommendations anywhere.

Diabolica continued, "But I'm also the kind of witch who knows *exactly* where you'll find your last recommendation..."

"You, become Most Superior High and Wicked Witch!" Helza screamed with laughter again. "Ohhhh that's funny," she added, just to make sure that Sam knew how funny it was. In case the laughter hadn't given it away.

Sam lifted Ringo to her shoulder. She muttered a few words and flicked her wand. She pointed towards a poster of the hottest boy band at the top of the charts. At once the boys in the poster began singing their latest hit. Helza stopped laughing and stared. Sam whirled and the skeletons climbed out of their chains and started to dance. She raised her hand and a flashing ball of lights appeared. Tapping her foot in time to the song, she spun the wand around her head. Ringo also tapped a couple of his feet in time with the music and helped her with the magic. The pop star boys climbed out of the poster and began dancing round Helza, whose mouth was open so wide that a passing caveman could have moved in.

Sam had become *very* good at magic, *very* quickly, which just goes to show what happens if you study hard.

The music got louder and the lights wilder. One of the pop star boys – Helza's favourite – leaned forward and kissed her on the cheek. "So, we were just talking about your recommending me for Most Superior High and Wicked Witch," Sam shouted over the noise.

Helza, was finding it difficult to speak. Her cheek

burned from the kiss and her knees had gone wobbly. Finally, she managed to stammer, "I...I'll, uh fetch a pen."

"And if you're so good at potions," Sam yelled, "do you have something that will really impress the judges at the trials?"

"I've got just what you need," Helza shouted back with a touch of awe in her voice. "It's brand new. No one has ever have seen it before. You'd better stand back."

"So we are agreed then, Mistress Sniff?" Diabolica asked. "I will recommend you as Most Superior High and Wicked Witch if you help me save the world from the evil vampire-witch."

Esmelia nodded her agreement. She didn't trust Diabolica at all, but that was nothing unusual. She hadn't trusted anyone since, well... ever.

Diabolica signed the thick, yellow paper with a great flourish and handed it to Esmelia. "With my very best wishes," she smiled.

*Witches and Wizard of the judging panel,*

*I hereby recommend Esmelia Sniff as Most Superior High and Wicked Witch. I can't begin to*

*list her fine quality or her talents as a witch. I am
sure she will be just as bad as the last stupid old
crone, if not slightly worse.*

*Signed
Diabolica Nightshade*

Esmelia stared at it in triumph. She could feel a
cackle coming on. And the weather was perfect for it, too.
It was funny, though, the more she stared at the paper, the
more it looked like the signature said "Deadly"
Nightshade. Oh well, she told herself. Who cares a
tiddler's bum how the vain baggage signs her name? She
tucked the parchment into her vest and made a mental
note to have Diabolica thrown into a scorpion pit once
she was Most Superior High and Wicked Witch. Saving
the world could become a bit of a habit and what if she
decided to save the world from Esmelia Sniff? No,
Diabolica Nightshade, or whatever she called herself,
would be much safer at the bottom of a large hole filled
with poisonous insects.

Sam stopped the music when Helza swooned into the
arms of the pop star boy. By the time she opened her eyes

the older girl declared herself Sam's best friend, like forever. Five minutes later she passed the younger apprentice a note scrawled on a scrap of paper. It read:

*Dear lame brain old bags and dull wizard*

*I recommend Sam as Most Superior High and Wicked Witch because she is totally awesome. I mean you should see some of the stuff she can do. It's totally going to blow your boring old minds.*

*Love n kisses*
*Helza Poppin*

"You will remember me, won't you?" Helza asked, handing over a packet of potion recipes, which Sam tucked away in her bag.

Sam nodded. "Of course. When I've won, making Diabolica let you go will be the first thing I do."

Sam and Esmelia had gone and Diabolica was laying on the sofa stroking Mr Popsy. It had been even easier to fool Esmelia than she'd thought. The wart-faced, oven-door-slamming, cauldron-mumbler had swallowed her story and would now do everything she told her too. And then she, Diabolica Nightshade, would raise an army of witches and take over the world. She sighed and relaxed deeper into the cushions. There was something about the apprentice though that nagged at the back of her mind. She looked up.

"What did you think of Esmelia's apprentice, Igor?" Diabolica asked.

Helza's eyes narrowed. "Didn't bother talking to her, she was boring," she muttered in reply.

"Did you think so? *I* thought she was rather *interesting*. There's power there. She'd be pretty, too, with a good wash and some decent clothes."

"What*ever*," replied her unwilling apprentice.

"Oh, go back to your dungeon and your silly potions Igor."

Once Helza had left the room, Diabolica held the kitten up to her face and kissed it. "Isn't Igor rude, Mr Popsy? Should we kill her do you think? And take Esmelia's apprentice instead?" She sighed once more. "Maybe another day when we're less busy. Right now mumma's got lots to do planning to be Most Superior High and Wicked Witch and after that the fun really begins. There's no rest for the wicked."

# 18 *Meeep!*

"We're going home then?" Sam asked as they flew through the starry night.

"Yes," snapped Esmelia from the front of the broom while cleaning out her ear with a little finger (Sam was disgusted to see that it wasn't her own little finger). "But we're stopping at Bridlington-on-Sea first." She finished cleaning out her ear, sucked the wax off the dried finger and popped back it into a pocket deep inside her cloak.

The old witch pushed the broom to its top speed, so it was still dark by the time they were nearly at their destination. Esmelia pulled up sharply. "Bridlington," she muttered, scratching her chin, "Fiddlington, Widdlington, *Bridlington*... Oh yes, thattaway."

A few minutes later the broomstick landed in bushes outside a large, redbrick house that was leaning over the edge of a cliff, as if trying to decide whether to jump off or not. Sam, who had spent her whole life in an orphanage, could tell at a glance that this was not someone's home. A sign beside the path leading up to the door told her she was right. It read:

## THE WICKEDEST WITCH

'The Lady Incontena Home for Old Ladies (who might be a bit peculiar but are definitely NOT witches whatever people might say.)'

Underneath, in smaller writing, it said:

"We are proud to say that we do *not* smell of boiled cabbage."

And beneath that in even smaller writing it said, "Sorry about all the other smells though."

"What are we doing at an old peoples' home?" Sam asked.

The old witch tapped her nose. "Esmelia's little secret dearie," she said mysteriously. "You stay right here. Do not leave these bushes. Do not follow me, peer in any windows, or otherwise spy on me, or I'll make balloon animals with your insides. Right?"

Sam nodded. Esmelia turned and walked towards the door of the Lady Incontena Home for Old Ladies. Having counted to five, Sam crept up to the house and started peering in windows with just a tiny twinge of guilt. She knew she had promised Esmelia that she wouldn't, but she *was* practicing being nasty. At the seventh window she saw the door to the room inside open a crack and Esmelia look in.

In the dim light, surrounded by cobwebs, Sam saw what she thought must be the oldest person in the world.

A tiny, bird-like figure who looked as though she might crumble into dust if you breathed on her too heavily. She was sitting in a big chair with an old knitted blanket on her knees. On her head was balanced a slice of bread.

As Sam watched, Esmelia tiptoed across the floor and poked the old woman hard in the ribs. She shrieked "Meeep!" and the chair fell over backwards. (If you listen very closely, you will hear that "meep" is the sound a cheese sandwich makes when startled.)

Laying on her back with her legs in the air, the old lady looked up and saw the ghastly face of Esmelia Sniff looming above her. Sam thought she would scream or make the horrible "Meeep" noise again, but instead she smiled. Through the half-open window Sam heard her say, "Why, it's little Esmelia!"

"Nanna Wonk," Esmelia replied. "Not being dead just now then?"

"Oh no, dearie. They buried me last time. In a coffin if-you-please. Without even asking! I had to tunnel my way out with a pickled cucumber."

While Nanna Wonk talked, Esmelia righted her chair and helped her arrange the bread on her head.

"Oooh I haven't been poked like that in such a long time," Nanna said. "You always was a good poker, Esmelia dear…"

"Nanna," Esmelia interrupted, rubbing her hands together. "I wonder if I might ask a tiny little favour? Just for old times' sake."

"After a poke like that you can ask me anything. Do you remember when them rats ate your bed? How we laughed. You slept on the wardrobe for years after. That'll teach her, I remember saying to myself. There's a girl who will always know how to catch forty winks on top of a wardrobe…" Nanna was old and old people always tend to go on a bit if you get them started.

"Just a tiny little favour Nanna," Esmelia wheedled, waving a sheet of paper before the old witch's face.

Ten minutes later Esmelia left the Lady Incontena Home. She was almost skipping as she crossed the lawn to where Sam stood waiting by the broom. With two recommendations she only needed Sam to pass her test and she was on her way to Transylvania and into the history books as the 173rd Most Superior High and Wicked Witch.

Sam only had two recommendations. Nevertheless, she, too, was smiling.

# 19 Agracadabra

They'd been sat in the chilly waiting room of the Apprentice Witch Testing Centre for hours and Sam was getting more and more nervous. For the past week she and Ringo had sat in her attic room memorizing every spell in Esmelia's books plus a few more that Lilith Dwale had taught them. She had practised making potions until her own eyebrows turned green with the fumes (luckily this had worn off after a few hours) and swooped across the sky every night on the broom until she felt like she could ride through a hurricane. She was ready. Yet still it felt like her legs had turned into jelly. (She'd checked them to make sure they hadn't, you couldn't be too careful with Esmelia around.) Sam had heard of having butterflies in your stomach, but hers felt more like a flock of bats were having a party. She'd had to go to the toilet eight times. Plus Esmelia was really getting on her nerves.

"It don't matter if you're not much good," the crone prattled, "You ain't really a proper witch. Just try and do *some* kind of magic and give it a good cackle, the examiners will like that. If you get really stuck you can always try shouting 'Agracadabra' and pulling a hankie out your sleeve. It might work." She passed Sam a hankie that had obviously been no stranger to a snotty nose. It was the crunchiest piece of material Sam had ever seen. Under Esmelia's beady gaze she pushed it up her sleeve, trying not to let disgust show on her face or touch the hankie too much.

Beside them sat half a dozen other witches with their apprentices, all of whom were making a point of ignoring them. Some hid behind copies of the latest *Cackler,* which seemed to have lost interest in Esmelia since they returned from their travels. Today's headline read:

*TRIALS START TOMORROW: VON DRAKULA TIPPED TO BE NEW HEAD HONCHO.*

Outside, young witches shot through the air on broomsticks. There was the occasional scream and Sam was pleased to see out the window that some of the girls were zipping around the sky upside down.

Eventually Sam's name was called by a witch with grey hair in a tight bun, a clipboard and a nose so snooty it pointed to the ceiling. Esmelia gave her apprentice a final poke and whispered, "Come back a witch or you'll be straight into the saucepan. It's up to you." Then Sam was led away into a small grey room.

"Good afternoon," the grey-haired witch said sharply. "I am the chief examiner here. My name is Mistress Wellingtonia Smellie-Dogbasquet and you are…" She checked he clipboard. "Ah yaaas, Samantha. Apprenticed to Esmelia Sniff, I believe?"

Sam nodded. "It's just Sam," she said. "Samantha sounds like an old man coughing."

Wellingtonia Smellie-Dogbasquet snorted rudely. "Well, *Samantha* we won't expect much of *you*. I understand the witch Sniff – if you can call her a witch – took you on just so that you could give her a recommendation for the Most Superior High and Wicked Witch trials. Very bad show. Not the ticket at all."

Sam was getting a bit fed up of people thinking she'd be rubbish. Pulling her wand out of a pocket she tapped it on the table and said, "Shall we get started?"

Wellingtonia peered down her nose at Sam. "Yaaaas," she drawled. "But you won't be needing *that* just yet."

There was a row of brooms in a rack, each of them sleek with perfectly groomed bristles. Except one. The last broom had six twigs sticking out at odd angles and was bucking madly against heavy chains. As Wellingtonia Smellie-Dogbasquet strolled down the line, Sam felt the bats in her stomach start a fight. She really needed the toilet again.

"Oh what a *dreadful* shame," smiled the examiner, stopping beside the furious broomstick. "It looks like this is the only one left in your size. It's just the *teensiest* bit lively, but I'm sure that won't be a problem, will it?"

Sam stepped forward and grabbed the stick as Wellingtonia turned a key in the padlock. The chains dropped away and the broom made a break for it, tossing and fighting Sam to get away. Using all her strength, she just about managed to wrestle it to the floor.

Ignoring the commotion, Wellingtonia began giving Sam instructions, "I want you to fly up to three thousand feet in a spiral, then give me six loop the loops with an emergency stop at the top of each, a three point turn and come down backwards."

All the other apprentice witches were being asked to fly across a field in a straight line and then come back again. "But that's not fair!" Sam panted, still struggling with the broom.

The examiner added, "And you're not to use your hands."

"But…"

"One more word and you'll be blindfolded too," the witch said in a voice as silky as a millionaire's pyjamas.

Sam gritted her teeth and muttered to the broom quickly. Telling it she'd take an axe to it made it worse. She fought to keep it under control, but it was going to throw her off any moment.

"You have ten seconds to start," Wellingtonia said. Sam was beginning to see why Esmelia liked to poke other witches in the eye.

She grasped the broom tighter and tried to feel the magic within.

"Ten," said the examiner.

There it was; gently fizzing.

"Nine."

Sam closed her eyes and concentrated.

"Eight."

It was a strange spell; much different to the one in Esmelia's broom. A spell that had only ever been cast once, by the witch who had made it.

"Seven."

And the witch had bound it to her. This broom had been made for one rider and one rider only. Being used by so many had made the magic confused and angry.

"Six."

With her mind Sam tried to soothe the broom. It twisted to smash her on the head.

"Five."

She tried again, but it began bucking even harder, trying to get away.

"Four." There was a smirk in the examiner's voice.

Sam had an idea. She held the broom tightly and screwed her eyes up.

"Three."

With every bit of concentration she had, Sam threw one thought down through her hands and into the heaving broom: "Be mine."

"Two."

It stopped jumping. The magic in it seemed to flow up Sam's arms and into her brain, joining the two of them forever. "Be mine," she thought as hard as she could. "Be mine, be mine, be mine."

"On..."

The broomstick swept between Sam's legs and carried her into the air at a speed that made Esmelia's look like a flying snail. Whoever had cast the spell had been amazingly, outstandingly good at magic. Sam didn't need her hands. She didn't even need to sit properly. This broom would never let her fall. It would take her anywhere she wanted to go. Anywhere. In this world or any other. She could feel it: this broom *loved* her.

She spiralled up into the air and at exactly three thousand feet swished into a graceful loop the loop. At the top Sam tucked a leg underneath and when it stopped she hung for a moment, not feeling in the slightest bit scared, but making sure her hat didn't fall off. While the broom completed another five loops she studied her fingernails. A quick three point turn and they returned to the ground, backwards, gently floating down to where Wellingtonia Smellie-Dogbasquet stood, looking aghast.

Sam hovered next to her. "Would you like me to do it blindfolded now?" she asked sweetly.

And that would have been really cool, but Sam had another question and it had to be asked. "Can I use the toilet, like right now?" she said. Which ruined it, really.

The rest of the test was easy. It was almost as if the chief examiner hadn't expected Sam to pass the broomstick flying so hadn't prepared any other nasty surprises. The bats in Sam's stomach all seemed to have gone and she whistled happily while she mixed up one of Helza Poppin's simpler potions, performed a couple of spells and cursed a large turnip until it melted and dripped off

the table. Ringo scurried about helping and, when
the boggle-eyed witch wasn't looking, making rude
beetle gestures at her with his front legs.

However much Wellingtonia scoffed and
made nasty remarks and scowled she had no
choice but to put ticks in all the right
boxes. Eventually, she led Sam to a desk
where another witch, who was about
two foot high and two foot round,
issued her with a full witch's licence
and papers saying that Ringo was
an official familiar. The little

beetle did somersaults on Sam's shoulder and turned his shiny back turquoise flecked with gold. Sam told him it was very dashing.

And that was it. Her licence was stamped and handed over the counter and she was a witch. A proper witch. Sam felt a quiet glow of joy. There was just one more thing.

"Mistress Smellie-Dogbasquet?"

"What now?"

"That old broom with the six twigs that tries to throw you off. I'd really like it."

"That's Apprentice Witch Testing Centre property," Wellingtonia replied with a sneer, "It's out of the question..."

"You never mean that one do you?" squeaked the tiny witch behind the counter. She was standing on a chair and pointing out the window.

Sam nodded.

"Oooo, it's a bad one that one. Any examiner using that one would be in big trouble, isn't it Mistress Smellie-Dogbasquet? It was supposed to have been thrown out yonks ago."

"Oh, take the stupid broom if you want it," Wellingtonia snarled and stalked off.

Esmelia was in the waiting room doing the crossword in *The Cackler.* "3 Across," she read. "What Esmelia Sniff smells of; three letters." She looked down. First letter was a "W" then there was a blank and the third letter was "E." Hmm, she thought; a tricky one. When Sam walked in she glanced up. The new witch flashed her shiny licence, grinning from ear to ear. She seemed to be expecting Esmelia to say something. The old witch wondered what.

"Well done," Sam prompted her.

"Why, what've I done?"

"Not you, me."

"Oh, did you kill someone?"

Sam sighed. She should know the silly crone better by now she supposed. "I've got my own broom too," she said, holding it out.

"It's going bald," Esmelia sniffed.

A few minutes later they were in the air, preparing to fly home, when Sam spotted Wellingtonia Smellie-Dogbasquet walking below.

"Hang on a second," she shouted at Esmelia. Her broom darted away until it was hovering just above the examiner.

"Mistress Smellie-Dogbasquet, I've got another spell to show you," Sam shouted down.

The examiner glared up at her and sneered, "What spell?"

"Agracadabra," Sam yelled, pulling Esmelia's hanky from her sleeve. The face below was showered in dried up old bogies. Wellingtonia Smellie-Dogbasquet yelped and shook a fist at the empty air. Sam flew away, cackling.

Esmelia stared at her apprentice. Maybe she'd been wrong, she thought. Maybe the little maggot had the makings of a witch after all. That had been quite *nasty*. She felt almost, what was the word? Oh yes: *proud*.

# 20 *Esmelia 3 — Sam 2*

"Sit!"

Sam sat. Esmelia dropped a sheet of paper and a pen on the kitchen table before her. "Now write this down," the old witch commanded. She paced around the table. "I think

Esmelia Sniff would make a fantastic Most Superior High and Wicked Witch because…"

Sam sucked the end of the pen. Should she write it? She had Ringo and a licence and her broom and she was sure she was already better at magic than Esmelia. There was no reason why she should, was there?

"Get on with it then you little worm."

And yet… Esmelia had given her a hat and a wand. Although she hadn't exactly *helped* much, Sam wouldn't be a witch now if it weren't for her. And whatever else you could say about her, she'd had more fun with Esmelia in the last three weeks than she'd had in her whole life. Besides, when you came right down to it, she was Esmelia's apprentice and that ought to count for something.

She started writing.

"…plus she's oodles better than them other witches and deserves to be allowed to jump around on them singing the 'Ain't You Got a Flat Head Now?' song." Esmelia finished and glared at Sam. "Get all that?"

Sam nodded and copied it down in her best handwriting.

Ten minutes later the apprentice escaped to her room so she didn't have to listen to Esmelia's mad cackling, which was irritating, but not so much as the singing:

*You think you're so wow,*
*that you're the best anyhow*
*So I've put on my boots*
*then jumped up and down*
*And my my my my, but ain't you got a flat*
*head nowwww!*

Sam packed her rucksack, making sure her two recommendations were safely tucked inside, then placed her broom on a chest by her bed. With twigs taken from the other old broomsticks and some old tools she'd found in a box, she carefully repaired it while Ringo walked up and down the handle polishing with a tiny cloth. By the time they'd finished, the broom was clipped, shining and looked like it was built for speed. As an added bonus it was also really good at sweeping dust out of hard-to-get-to corners.

Delighted with her new broom, Sam turned it over to inspect it from every angle. As she did so something caught her eye. Tiny scratches. She looked closely. It was writing. "This broom belongs to Lilith Dwale," she read. As she did so, the writing changed. Now it read, "This broom belongs to Sam." On the desk *Think Yourself Witch* shuffled itself, sounding happy.

She picked up the book. Something had been

bothering her for a while and the broom was the last straw. "Why?" she asked it. "Why are you helping me like this? And how come I've got your broom? What's going on here?"

Opening a page at random, Sam found ordinary notes on interior design for witches. The words stubbornly refused to change no matter how many times she repeated the questions, though Sam was sure she heard a very faint laugh.

Rapping the page with her knuckles, she asked one last time and now the spidery writing across the page began to disappear and reform. The page read:

*It begins tomorrow. Be <u>nasty</u>.*

No amount of questioning, cajoling or throwing the book down in a huff would make it change. The message from Lilith stayed exactly the same. Eventually, Sam closed it and shrugged. When she was Most Superior High and Wicked Witch she would find out everything there was to know about Lilith Dwale. In the meantime she had a competition to win. She climbed into bed and by the light of a flickering candle checked that she now knew every spell in Esmelia's books. Ringo kindly turned the pages for her.

# 21 The Bleak Fortress

As usual when there was travelling to be done, Esmelia was banging on the ceiling just as Pigsnout Wood's night creatures were licking the blood off their claws and settling down for a well-earned rest. The early bird, meanwhile, was fluffing out its feathers and thinking that it might be nice to go a-hunting for worms before all the other birds got there and ruined it.

The old witch needn't have bothered with her banging. Sam had been far too excited to get more than a few snatched moments of sleep and was already up, washed and dressed in her best clothes. It meant wearing her dress, which she hated, but Esmelia was right: with the black, pointed hat it did look a lot more witchy. And today, of all days, was a good day to look as much like a witch as possible. She tapped Ringo's back until he woke up, allowed him a very quick set of press-ups and walked down the stairs carrying her new broom and rucksack.

"Is that a *dress*?" cackled Esmelia while rubbing her hands together. "Ain't you the proper old-fashioned witch, eh?" For once the old witch didn't give Sam a look of sneering disapproval mixed with barely disguised hunger, though she still pushed her out the door with more poking than was necessary. Then they were off, the two brooms climbing high into the pink dawn and racing south.

That is to say Sam raced and Esmelia puttered along on her Bumsling, Moidor and Wibble broom, which was supposed to be the fastest model in the world. Sam had to keep reminding her own broom to slow down and even then there were dozens of times when she had to stop and wait for the tiny, scowling black dot behind them to catch up. But gradually they flew closer and closer to Transylvania. Sam began to see other broomsticks headed in the same direction, looking like flocks of migrating birds. Slowly, the sky was getting darker, too. Ahead, black clouds spat lightening at each other.

Into the storm they headed and now tall, jagged mountains surrounded them. Caught in the thickening flock of flying witches, Sam and Esmelia steered this way and that through the forest of black, razor-sharp peaks. Suddenly, there was a huge crash of thunder. In front, Sam saw lightening flash from a cloud and touch what she had thought was a mountain peak. In the brief burst of light she saw that she had been wrong. It was a turret. Clinging to the top of a mountain was a huge castle of spires and battlements and forbidding grey walls. Parts were in ruins and weird lights flickered at slit windows. As Sam watched, open mouthed, a massive cloud of bats burst from one of the towers.

"The Bleak Fortress," cackled Esmelia. Unseen, she had pulled her broom alongside Sam's. "The black heart of witchcraft. Built over a thousand years ago in the Gloomic Style, for Gruselda the Skanky. Every bedroom's got an en suite torture chamber, there's bats in the belfry, rats in the dungeons and dreadful oozing things in the secret passages. And in a couple of days it's all *mine*."

She snickered at Sam. "You'll be cleaning out the toilets. There's a hundred and twelve."

Sam flicked her an annoyed glance and found herself looking forward to Esmelia's expression when she found out that her apprentice would also be competing. Without a word, Sam pulled the broom round and followed the stream of other witches down towards the heavily forested valley over which the Bleak Fortress loomed. On the ground Sam could make out motorbikes, cars and even a tank making their way along the winding mountain road.

They joined the circling swirl of flying witches. Sam had never imagined there could be so many. It looked like witches from every corner of the world had arrived, along with the nooks and crannies of several other worlds. There were witches in swishing bright satins, witches in black lace, witches with tall hats, beautiful witches, ugly witches, young and old and everything in between. One shot by in a jangle of jewellery trailing long ribbons of black silk, another cackled past in a flying bathtub with shower attachment. A prim looking woman was flying under a large black umbrella.

Below them all was a wooden arena in a clearing, lit up by beams of magical light and surrounded by an enormous camp site made up of tents in every style, from pavilions of black silk to old blankets thrown over a convenient branch. From the stage organ music crashed loud enough to make Sam's teeth rattle and a spotlight lit up a tiny figure. It raised a microphone to its lips and then a familiar voice boomed:

"Welcome one and all! Welcome to the greatest show in the universe. The Bleak Fortress is proud to present the 173$^{rd}$ Trial for the Most Superior High and Wicked Witch. Over the next two days we'll be finding out which witch is up to scratch. Who's got the Hex Factor? I'm your host Diabolica Nightshade and the next three days are going to be WICKED!"

# 22 Let's Meet the Contestants

As the stormy gloom darkened into night, the clouds parted to reveal a fat full moon behind the Bleak Fortress. Wolves howled in the distance and by the steps leading up to the stage, Sam hopped from one foot to another in the shadows. Inside the arena, a sea of witches made their way to seats and argued with each other. Sam could hear hundreds of voices all saying pretty much the same thing: "Excuse me, would you mind removing your hat please I can't see a thing." Most, however, were not so polite. A number of fist, handbag and broom fights had already broken out. One witch with mad hair had a shoulder-mounted rocket launcher aimed at a hat two feet in front of her.

Just as things were threatening to get out of hand, the stage blazed with lights and loud music flooded the arena. Fireworks rocketed into the sky. In a spotlight stood Diabolica Nightshade.

The audience stopped fighting and cheered. Another witch took advantage of the distraction to chop the top off the hat in front with a pair of garden shears.

"Witches of the world," Diabolica said quietly, so every ear in the place strained to hear. "In a moment we'll meet the contestants. One of them will be your new Most Superior High and Wicked Witch. Not only will the lucky winner be presented with the Black Wand of Ohh Please Don't Turn Me Into Aaaaarghhh…Ribbett, the most powerful wand ever made, but she will rule over all witches everywhere from the Bleak Fortress itself. Over the next two days the contestants will be fighting for nothing less than a place in *history*!"

Diabolica paused for effect.

"And what a fight it's going to be!" Diabolica had raised her voice now. "But all that's to come. First let's meet the judges!"

The crowd howled their approval.

"Leader of the Grand Coven and Lady of the Mystic Cards of Fortune, it's only the one and only Tiffany Toadlick."

A spotlight picked out a witch in a sparkly black dress and hat who waved to the crowd. She was holding a little dog that would have been fluffy if most of its hair hadn't have fallen out. It licked her face. She licked it back.

"Ten times winner of the Warts and All Prize, a witch so ugly that she once turned her own nose into a toad and no one noticed. It's the witch who put the 'Ghhaaaaa!' in 'ghastly,' the "sick" in 'sickening'. Try not to throw up and give a warm welcome to Scary *Doris*!"

Another spotlight lit up a hunched figure in black rags. The audience screamed louder than ever. Doris was so fantastically gruesome that she made Esmelia look like a supermodel. She waved and one of her fingers dropped off.

# THE WICKEDEST WITCH

"And finally, for the first time ever, we have a wizard on the judges panel. But not just any wizard. He's *Playwitch* magazine's pinup of the year…Dr Sulfurus Cowl!"

A third spotlight shone on a wizard in spangly robes and a tall hat covered with stars and moons. He spun around, struck a pose, grinned at the audience and winked. Lights made pretty stars on his blindingly white teeth.

The crowd went mad. There were whistles and "phwwoaaars." Several witches threw their knickers at the wizard, who would have been scarred for life if he hadn't managed to dodge them all.

"But now the moment you've all been waiting for." Diabolica continued as the judges took their seats. "It's time to meet the contestants."

A large witch wearing a robe that said 'SECURITY' across the back pushed a skinny woman in a red white and blue striped pointy hat up the stairs towards Diabolica. She blinked under the lights for a moment and then walked forward scowling.

"All the way from France, it's Mad Elaine de la Moustache!" Diabolica shouted. "Let's see those recommendations Mad Elaine."

The French witch scowled even more deeply, spat and held out three pieces of paper. Diabolica quickly read through them. "Mad Elaine has been put forward by Peglette de Cochon, Boo Lala and Maman Leshrug. That all seems to be in order Mad Elaine. Who's next?"

Sam's gaped as the next witch waddled up the steps. It was Wellingtonia Smellie-Dogbasquet. Suddenly, it was clear why she had tried to stop Sam passing her test. If Sam hadn't been able to recommend Esmelia it would have meant one less witch in the competition. Sam stared at her. Some witches, she thought, really *are* horrid.

The next three witches Sam had never heard of. First was a small, bent witch with sharpened teeth and a necklace of human ears. Even from afar she made Sam shudder. Her name was Callous Meg. Second was a haughty witch in flowing robes, a crown of steel and a dead-looking raven on her shoulder. One of its eyeballs was hanging out. Diabolica introduced her as Queen Maligana. Last was a tall, white-haired lady in robes. She carried a carved staff and had strapped a pair of antlers to her head. Her name was Pagan Whickerman.

"Dunno what they let her type in for," Esmelia groaned. "It's not proper witchcraft stuffing people into giant men made out of sticks and setting them on fire." She paused. "I ain't saying it's not *fun* mind, but it ain't *proper* witchcraft."

She was cut short by the security witch prodding her towards the steps. After stopping to glare at the prodder, Esmelia put her chin in the air and was gone.

The spotlight shone on Esmelia as she strode towards the front of the stage. The audience went completely silent, then Diabolica shouted, "Give a huge welcome to Esmelia Sniff!"

At once the audience erupted in boos and jeers. There were whistles and catcalls. One witch, who was a little slow to catch on, threw her knickers at Esmelia.

"Rubbish," shouted another.

"Now now," Diabolica said. "The competition is open to all. And Esmelia has recommendations from, let's see… her apprentice Sam, who I hear passed her test yesterday, Nanna Wonk and your very own host Diabolica Nightshade. Well done Esmelia."

"Cheat," shouted someone.

"It's a fix," cried another.

"But we *like* cheating," bellowed a witch at the back.

Esmelia leered at the jeering crowd. Then she cackled. The cackle back at the cottage seemed like a girlish titter compared to this one. This cackle was long and full of phlegm and insane wickedness. It struck a chill into Sam's heart.

"Kiss my warts," Esmelia added when the final echo had rolled away. Then she made a very rude gesture at the stunned crowd. Diabolica caught her by the elbow and pulled her to the side of the stage.

"And now," shouted Diabolica. "I believe we have one more contestant…"

With rubber legs, Sam walked onto the stage.

"The dark mistress…"

Sam tugged at her sleeve.

Diabolica looked down. "Errr… Sam," she finished a bit lamely.

From the side of the stage, Esmelia hissed, "Gettoffoutofit you brainless little maggot," and ran on to snatch her apprentice away. A security witch grabbed her and pulled her back.

Diabolica looked down at Sam. "You shouldn't be up here," she whispered and pushed her away.

Sam pulled a face and two bits of paper from her vest.

The beautiful witch's face turned white. "You can't mean…?" she gasped.

Sam nodded.

Esmelia screeched. Out of the corner of her eye the apprentice could see her gnashing her teeth. Her hair was standing on end. Lilith knew what she was talking about, Sam thought. Nasty is a dish best served up with a good helping of surprise on the side. Esmelia looked as though she was going to explode at any second. For some reason though, Sam wasn't quite as gleeful as she thought she would be. Instead, she was a tiny bit ashamed of herself.

Diabolica meanwhile had regained her twinkling smile, though it looked strained. "Well, well well," she laughed at the audience. "A surprise entrant. Let's see shall we… A recommendation from Blanche Nightly, that's fine."

Esmelia screeched again. "You wait till I get my finger on you, you double-crossing, slimy little scumbag."

And one from…" Diabolica's face now went purple to match Esmelia's. "…*Igor*," she finally managed to splutter.

Then she was composed once more. "Oh, but what a shame. You need three. Nevermind, but let's have a big round of applause for the brave little girl."

The witches started clapping, then stopped just as quickly. Sam had pulled a book out of her rucksack. She tore out a page at random and gave it to Diabolica. The writing was already twisting into different letters. With disbelief in her voice, the host read out, "I, Lilith Dwale, recommend Sam as Most Superior High and Wicked Witch…"

She stopped and tried to get her breath.

"B…but she's dead," she spluttered, again. "There's

a rule. Rule 2652 section b, clause 3.""

At the side of the stage Tiffany Toadlick flicked through a large book until she found the right page. "Rule 2652 section b, clause 3," she read out. "No recommending witch may be *Fred*. Oh. I'm *sure* that's not what it said last week."

Even dead, Lilith Dwale was very very good at magic.

"Very well," snarled Diabolica Nightshade. "I hope you know what you're doing young lady." She pushed Sam towards the side of the stage where Esmelia had fainted. This time Sam allowed herself to be pushed. It couldn't be undone now; she was in the race to become Most Superior High and Wicked Witch. Two seconds later she wished she wasn't.

Behind her a mist crept over the stage and the evening suddenly seemed much much darker. The crowd went silent and Sam turned to see the mist thicken, become a column, which turned into the figure of a woman. Power crackled off her. She was tall and proud and ancient. Her eyes blazed with dark, wicked fire. She wore a long cloak lined with silk of blood red and someone had styled her hair so it looked like a large bum on top of her head. Sam felt her legs give way beneath her. How could she – a witch who had only passed her test yesterday – hope to stand against this great being. Even if Lilith was right and she was a natural, this witch looked as if she had been practicing for hundreds and hundreds of years. Sam bit her lip and the tiniest trickle of blood seeped out. At once, the witch at the front of the stage glanced round and for a single instant smiled at Sam, so she could see the flash of long, sharp fangs. Then Cakula von Drakula turned to the audience.

"Haff I missed somesing?" she asked. And then laughed, "Mwah, ha ha ha ha HAA!" As vampires do.

# 23 Circle of Power

There was barely time for Sam to be shown to her competitor's tent before the trials began. In the distance she could still hear Esmelia screeching in fury and tried not to listen to the horrible insults and threats. She had just finished unpacking the pink rucksack when the front flap was thrown back. There was a brief whirl of purple hair.

"Can't let Diabolica see me," Helza panted. "She's *totally* in a mood right now. Tried to turn my bones to gravy a minute ago."

"Are you OK?" Sam yelped.

Helza flapped a hand and tutted, "Invented a potion that makes me immune to magic." Her face broke into a broad grin. Sam noticed her friend was very pretty when she wasn't scowling. "You were *awesome*," she continued. "I thought Esmelia was going to have convulsions and Diabolica's face… I haven't laughed so hard since she accidentally poisoned herself."

Sam tried to smile, but it felt forced, so she let it go. "Actually, I felt a bit bad for Esmelia," she mumbled.

"One minute!" shouted a voice from outside the tent.

"You'd better go," said Helza. "Don't worry about Esmelia. She's one of those old-fashioned types, so she's supposed to *like* witches being nasty, right? You are a witch aren't you?"

Sam nodded.

"Well get out there and show them then."

Feeling slightly better, Sam went.

Diabolica swished across the stage. "Eight witches!" she cried. "After every trial one must go. First round is Transformation. They have ten minutes to turn each other into as many things as possible. Two points for every time they manage it and a point for every time they successfully block a spell. Apart from that, what are the rules Tiffany?"

Tiffany Toadlick stood up and shouted happily, "The rules are, there are no rules!"

"That's right," continued Diabolica. "Maybe they'll get turned back, maybe they won't…" She gave Sam a pointed look. "If it wasn't horribly dangerous everyone and their apprentice would be entering."

Sam grit her teeth. She felt the comforting tickle of Ringo at her neck and could feel him drawing power to her already. She felt her blood begin to tingle and the wand Esmelia had given her began to twitch.

"Wait for it…" shouted Diabolica. "In three, two, one, NOW!"

Sam barely saw Cakula move. She spun, her cloak swirling and her wand swept round in a circle, letting off seven spells so quickly they were almost simultaneous.

"An all-time classic from Cakula von Drakula," bellowed Diabolica. "And no blocks. That's fourteen points already."

Sam found that she was staring round at six frogs. She had a terrible urge to puff her neck up. Glancing down she saw webbed feet. 'Oh drat,' she thought. With the magic Ringo had gathered for her she repeated the counter spell in her head, croaked and was Sam again. She ducked as another of Cakula's spells whizzed at her. But now Callous Meg was back and evil-looking green trails of magic shot across the stage at the vampire-witch. All of them were easily blocked, but it kept Cakula busy for half a second while Sam drew her breath and looked round. The other witches were turning on each other. Out of the corner of her eye, she saw one frog twinkle back into the shape of Esmelia who turned on her instantly, her face lined with fury. A huge spell ripped from the old witch's fingers straight at her apprentice. Sam tried to block it, but it came on too fast. With a groan she found that she was now a maggot. Sam gathered her magic again, even as she furrowed her little maggot brow. Surely Esmelia didn't have so much power?

She became Sam again just as Pagan Whickerman next to her disappeared in a shower of glitter and became a small pastry. She heard Mad Elaine's laugh cut short as she puffed into a cloud of smoke that blew away to reveal a pumpkin.

"That's two points for Queen Maligana," Diabolica shouted.

By now flashing ribbons and balls of magic were streaming across the circle. Witch after witch flashed into different forms – a bat, a hatstand, a pottery unicorn – then changed back almost as quickly. Another spell from Esmelia hit Sam before she was even standing straight again. A slug this time and with each counter spell she was getting more tired.

"Five minutes gone and Cakula's clearly in the lead, followed by Esmelia," she heard Diabolica cry. "The apprentice, Sam has yet to score and it looks like she may be carried out on a lettuce leaf."

Sam shook herself back into her own body again and immediately turned to block Esmelia's next spell.

But Wellingtonia Smellie-Dogbasquet spread her fingers at Sam at exactly the same time. Her spell met Esmelia's and the two joined to create a sizzling orb of magic that was too strong for the apprentice witch. In a haze of shimmering lights she felt her body ripple with a painful twang and looked up with the eyes of an earwig.

Esmelia was cackling as she blocked spell after spell. Sam's brain felt like it was going to melt with the effort of countering. How could she have missed the fact that Esmelia was so good? Where was this magic coming from? As she stood again, she saw it. An almost invisible trail of dark light flowing from Diabolica's twitching fingers to Esmelia. Even as she watched, she saw Esmelia gather it up and shape it into a new spell. Esmelia and Diabolica were cheating!

Sam gasped and another spell hit her. She was a worm. Esmelia again, she guessed.

The Sam that stood this time was different. She was angry, exhausted, hurt and definitely not feeling sorry for Esmelia any more. In fact, she was feeling decidedly *nasty*. Yet another spell fizzed through the air at her. She scowled at it and slashed her wand, screaming "No!" It wasn't done properly, but the power behind the word was unstoppable. The transformation spell vanished.

"That's one point for Sam at last, but she'll have to

do better than that, she's well behind. Ooo there goes Wellingtonia again, she's now a small rubber duck for anyone who cares."

Again and again Sam drew magic to herself, with Ringo throwing in everything he could muster, but it wasn't enough. All she could do was block the spells coming at her thick and fast. The air was alive with them, the centre of the circle glowing as spells crossed each other, making the magic more and more unstable and dangerous. Witches were now turning into strange, unearthly creatures and it was costing Sam everything she had just to stop herself joining them.

"Thirty seconds," shouted Diabolica.

Sam grunted and blocked another spell that Esmelia hurled at her.

"Twenty."

So that was it, thought Sam as she flicked her wand at a stream of magic from Mad Elaine, she had no chance now.

There was a sharp pain at her neck. Ringo had pinched her! How could he do such a thing at a time like… And then Sam understood. She could still win this. With a surge of love for the little beetle she looked with fresh eyes into the circle.

"Ten."

She was drained. She felt like she had no magic left. Yet there was plenty in the circle, a blazing ball of it the size of a bush, created by the spells that were still coursing from witch to witch. All it would take was a burst at the centre.

Sam summoned magic one last time. An enormous amount of it. She let her anger take control again, raised her wand and sent it in a burning river straight to the centre of the circle.

The ball of magic exploded outwards, sending seven streams of raw blazing power out like the spokes of a wheel. The combined force of eight powerful witches.

"Aaaaand stop!" yelled Diabolica.

With a wet squelch the creature that had been Callous Meg tried to get up. It fell back, mewing in confusion. Sam stared around at the other beasts she had made. Feathers merged with scales and horrible slime. There were teeth and beaks and claws, but none was recognisable. Only Cakula von Drakula was untouched and even she seemed shocked at the strength of the spell.

The audience was silent. A minute passed. Two.

"Well, I make that twelve points for Sam," said Diabolica eventually. There was something like respect in her voice.

Sam threw herself on the camp bed groaning. She had just made it through to the next round, beating Pagan Whickerman by one point. Now that her fury had evaporated she couldn't help wondering if it was worth it. It had taken six highly trained witches to turn all the contestants back and they said Pagan would always have a small beak somewhere you wouldn't expect to find one. Was this what she had learned magic for? Sam asked herself while burying her face in the pillow. Betraying the person she was supposed to help? Throwing Esmelia's dried snot over people and turning other witches into unspeakable beasts? It wasn't right. She wasn't cut out to be nasty.

"That was pretty good," said Helza who had been sitting at the end of the bed when Sam entered. "And it's potions next. If you're using my recipe you're *so* going to win that."

With her eyes closed, Sam whispered, "Diabolica and Esmelia are cheating."

"I did wonder," replied her friend. "Diabolica's been collecting ingredients for a potion. She thinks I don't know she's got them hidden in her underwear drawer.

Why would she need them?"

Sam thought for a second. "Well, she's helping Esmelia and it's the potions trial tomorrow, so it looks like they're planning to cheat again. But why? What does Diabolica care if Esmelia wins or loses?"

"Who knows? But I've got an idea that might help us find out," said Helza with a grin. "You get some rest, I'll take care of this one."

# 24 Boil and Bubble

On the stage were seven work benches complete with cauldrons, each with its own fire burning merrily beneath. Seven witches stood behind. If looks could kill Sam would have been a small, smoking hole in the floor. She tried to ignore Esmelia and instead peeked at Cakula von Drakula.

The vampire-witch wore heavy veils and gloves to protect her from the morning sun. She stood completely still, but on the screen at the back of the stage her shadow was moving. Sam's eyes widened as she saw its dark hands moving, making shapes: rabbit, dog,

butterfly, screaming victim with bitten throat …

"Seven witches, all hoping to be Most Superior High and Wicked Witch," Diabolica bellowed as she strutted out onto the stage. "But only six can make it through to the next round. In a moment we'll find out who can mix the true brew, the supersonic tonic – but first let's speak to our fabulous judges."

The crowd cheered and Diabolica shushed them with a wave of her hand. "Tiffany," she said. "Any predictions?"

Tiffany Toadlick shuffled a deck of cards and laid some out on the table.

"The cards say there's a pirate coming with a bag of bananas," she squeaked.

"Thanks Tiff," Diabolica said, rolling her eyes. "Doris?"

"I had a penguin with one o' them. It went mwerk, mwerk, mwerk," screeched Scary Doris.

"Marvellous," replied Diabolica. "What do you think Dr. Cowl?"

The wizard was puffed up with self-importance, "Well, if you want my opinion…" he began.

"Not really," Diabolica interrupted. "I'm just filling in time."

She turned to the contestants and yelled into her microphone. "You have half an hour to give us your best potion in three… two… one… GO!"

Sam tipped her little bag of ingredients out on the table. Out of the corner of her eye she could see the other witches do the same. Cakula von Drakula's arms were a blur as she peeled, sliced, chopped and diced with superhuman speed. Mad Elaine had poured out a huge mound of garlic and was crushing it into her cauldron. The other witches were equally busy. Except Esmelia. All she seemed to be doing was boiling water calmly, giving it a lazy stir now and again.

Sam had no time to think about it and bent her head over her own pile. First chop the old man's glint, she reminded herself and then ten stings of bees that had only ever collected pollen by moonlight from white roses, a spoonful of newts' eyes, of course. And watch it bubble.

After a few minutes she became aware of someone leaning over her. She looked up and saw Diabolica.

"I've no idea what Sam is making," the host said into her microphone. "But it's green and bubbling and there's smoke coming off the top so who cares."

She winked at Sam and moved along to the next work-bench where she continued her commentary. "Queen Maligana seems to be doing something with snake heads and spider venom."

There was a pause. "Callous Meg's potion looks like, eeeuuurrgh."

Diabolica seemed to have moved on quickly. "And unless I'm very much mistaken," she continued "Esmelia is making a very fine quality Potion of Incredible Strength."

Glancing up Sam saw Diabolica lean over Esmelia's boiling water as if smelling it. A white shape, like a large teabag rolled down the brim of her hat and plopped into the cauldron. It was filled with potion ingredients. At once, rainbows sparkled above the cauldron.

Sam almost forgot her own potion at a critical moment when the baby's breath needed adding. She corrected the brew and allowed herself a smile. Diabolica *was* very much mistaken. Helza had stolen her potion ingredients and substituted the ingredients for a Truth

Brew. Until it wore off anyone who drank it could never lie. With any luck, Esmelia would soon be telling everyone in the arena why she and Diabolica were cheating. In the meantime, Sam stopped listening and concentrated on her cauldron, until she heard the host shout "And three… two… one, stop brewing please."

Sam threw her last ingredient into the pot, the wing of a mayfly freshly hatched. She remembered just in time to stand back. All around nature seemed to stand still. It drew a deep breath. And from every corner of Transylvania magic poured into her cauldron. There was a burst of white fire and a flock of doves burst out. And then silence.

# 25 The Queen is Dead

"Wheww, looks like Sam's cooked up a doozy," said Diabolica to the crowd. "Let's see how they did, shall we?"

When the applause finished Diabolica was standing by Wellingtonia Smellie-Dogbasquet's bench with a glass tube of silvery liquid in her hand.

"What's it do, Wellingtonia?" she asked.

"Yaaas," Wellingtonia sneered. 'It's my own invention. I call it the Potion of Health and Efficiency. One spoonful has the same effect as a brisk five mile walk followed by a cold shower and half a grapefruit."

Diabolica put her hand to her mouth and yawned. "Sounds great Wellingtonia," she said tossing the potion over her shoulder. "We'll take your word for it. Well done."

She approached Mad Elaine de la Moustache and took a step back when she got within six feet of the bench. "Whoa, Elaine," she gasped. "Just a little bit of garlic?"

Cakula von Drakula was also edging as far away from the French witch as possible.

"Oui," replied Mad Elaine. "Eet is mashed garlic, drizzled weeth syrup of garlic weeth just a peench of garlic. I call eet, ze Potion… of *Garlic*."

"But that's not magical, is it?"

The French witch took a swig from her glass beaker then walked over to a pot plant at the side of the stage, opened her mouth wide and breathed on it, with a HUUUURRRR sound. At once the plant shrivelled and died. Mad Elaine looked round. "You want to see what eet does to ze vampire?" she asked.

Under her veils Cakula looked stony. Diabolica moved on hurriedly.

The vampire-witch had served up a Potion of Steaming Desire. Sam could see smoky red love hearts drifting off the cauldron. The audience clapped politely.

"Maligana, what have *you* got?" Diabolica asked peering into her cauldron.

"Potion of Total Paralysis," the icy queen answered, "Good for coating apples with for those hard-to-kill princesses. One spoon and they sleep for ten minutes. Five spoons and they won't move for a century."

"Rubbish," came a dry, hoarse little voice, "That's only in stories." Callous Meg's eyes were twinkling with evil mischief. "Prove it."

Queen Maligana looked outraged, "How dare you, you filthy little beggar," she hissed.

Callous Meg bared her sharpened teeth. "You ain't

even a proper evil queen," she giggled. "Everyone knows you live in a caravan."

The queen raised her wand, her face thunderous. "It's a palace," she said through clenched teeth.

"On wheels," insisted Callous Meg.

Across the stage, Sam could feel Queen Maligana summoning magic and saw her muttering the words of a vicious curse. Tiffany interrupted. Holding the book of rules, she stood and said, "Actually, any competitor *is* allowed to ask for a demonstration."

Unsurprisingly, there were no volunteers to take Queen Maligana's potion. Finally the regal witch lost patience. "I'll take it myself," she scowled. "Watch. One drop and I'll sleep for a hundred seconds."

Callous Meg's eyes sparkled. Not for the first time, Sam felt a shiver of fear just looking at her.

With utmost care, Queen Maligana dropped a tiny amount of her potion onto her tongue and instantly fell into a deep sleep from which only the kiss of a handsome prince could awake her. Sadly, no one had thought to bring a handsome prince along.

Without a word Callous Meg took a spoonful of her own potion. "I think I'd like to demonstrate *my* potion now," she rasped in her dry voice. "What's the rules say about tryin' it on another competitor?"

Tiffany licked her finger and leafed through the pages. "It's fine, so long as they don't object," she answered.

Callous Meg looked down at Queen Maligana's sleeping form and hugged herself. Her chest heaved with laughter. "That's what I thought," she whispered. Then louder, she asked "Maligana, may I try this potion on you?"

She looked round at the audience. Every witch was holding her breath. "Anyone hear her object?" Meg giggled.

There was silence. Callous Meg darted round the bench and poured a spoonful of potion into Maligana's sleeping mouth. For a moment nothing happened and then the queen melted into a wriggling mass of centipedes and maggots and other horrid bugs that scuttled away.

The crowd burst into applause. *This* was more like it. Meg bowed, her lips curled into a spiteful smile. Diabolica looked at Sam, "You see, my dear," she whispered. "It's not a game for little girls." Then she turned to the audience. "Did I say *seven* witches? I meant *six*!"

There was a howl of glee. Diabolica smirked and continued, "Let's see what's in Sam's pot."

Unable to take her eyes off the mess of creeping things that had been a witch only a few seconds ago, Sam lowered a beaker into her cauldron. It came out full of liquid that shone with a clear white light. "It's a n-new potion," she stammered. "Never been seen before. I-I'll n-need a volunteer, too. Someone old. I p-promise they won't be harmed."

Diabolica whirled around, "Well, who better than one of our very own judges. Doris, how about it?"

"I mugged him down a back alley,' shouted Scary Doris happily. "And told him I'd chew his elbows off next time."

"I think that's a 'yes'," said Diabolica leading Sam over to the judging panel. Sam offered up the glass to the hideous old hag, who swallowed it down in one gulp.

Instantly, Doris was surrounded by a white glow. Her skin began to melt. "Weeeek," she cried. "Polly slammed me toes in the drawer."

The light grew brighter and brighter until it was impossible to see the old witch at its centre. Then, suddenly, it blinked out.

Where Scary Doris had sat was a stunning young woman. Her skin glowed like spring petals, white-blonde hair fell to her waist, her lips were the colour of ripe strawberries and her figure... Well, Dr Sulfurus Cowl was staring at her with his eyes bulging.

"I see," said Not-So-Scary-Now Doris, holding up a smooth hand to inspect it. "Some sort of Time Potion is it? Turns back the years?"

Sam nodded. Doris's gorgeous face wrinkled into a pretty frown. "Well, it better wear off in time for the next Warts and All Prize, young lady."

She should have been jubilant, but Sam returned to her bench just feeling slightly sick. In the front row Mandy Snoutley sucked her pencil and glared at her like a wolf that had just seen a lamb. A lamb carrying a sign saying, 'I'm Plump, Tender and Juicy, Just the Way that Wolves Love.'

"Well that just leaves the Potion of Incredible

Strength," Diabolica said to the crowd. She strolled over to Esmelia's bench.

The old witch was still glowering at Sam. She'd never even heard of a potion like that, she was thinking, let alone made one. How did the treacherous little cockroach find the recipe? When she got her hands on her...

"Esmelia?" Diabolica's voice prodded.

Without taking her eyes off Sam, Esmelia dipped a cup into her cauldron, lifted it to her lips and swallowed. Right, she decided; now she was super strong she'd sneak into Cakula's tent later as she had arranged with Diabolica and give the vampire-witch's heart a good poking with the pointed stick. But there was more than enough time for that before the potion wore off. Enough time that she could first pull the maggoty little apprentice's arms off and beat her round the head with them. Right now though, she'd give the slimy little backstabber a piece of her mind. She opened her mouth.

Sam leaned forward.

Esmelia gave Sam her most vicious scowl and yelled...

"Last night I spent two hours peeking under Sulfurus Cowl's tent so I could watch him getting undressed."

The crowd fell about laughing. Esmelia clapped her hands over her mouth and ran off the stage. Dr. Sulfurus Cowl blushed and nudged his chair a little closer to Doris's. Sam groaned. Alright, she was angry with Esmelia for cheating and the old witch *was* planning to eat her, but Sam almost, kind of, sort of, *liked* her anyway. She hadn't meant for Esmelia to be so completely humiliated.

Diabolica watched the old witch go with a look of murderous fury. Her fingers curled as if she were choking the life out of someone.

The crowd was laughing so hard that no one noticed the host had stopped talking. After a few moments Diabolica pulled herself together and Sam watched her force a smile onto her face. "My mistake, looks like it was a Truth Brew after all," she smirked into the audience. "An excellent one though. Good job Esmelia, wherever you are. So which one of our contestants is going to be voted off? It's up to you now judges."

"If I'm *honest*," said Sulfurus Cowl, looking along the row of witches on stage. "I thought those were *great* potions, really amazing…"

"Oh, just get on with it," Diabolica cut in. She looked like she wanted to get off the stage as quickly as possible.

"OK, I've made a decision," he continued. "I'm going to send home Wellingtonia Smellie-Dogbasquet."

"Oh I hate this bit," said Doris, with the huge smile of someone who didn't really hate it at all. "But Sulfurus is right, Wellingtonia's potion was pants."

Tiffany consulted her cards, humming and haaing. "The cards are in agreement with Doris and Sulfurus," she nodded. She looked again, confused. "And also they say there's a witch-child here. But that *can't* be right can it? Witches aren't allowed to have children. It's completely against the law."

Diabolica's face was stony. She ignored Tiffany and turned to where a sobbing Wellingtonia Dagbasquet was slumped over her bench. "That's three votes Wellingtonia. I'm going to have to ask you to leave. You're out, clear off, you're cluttering up the stage."

Sam didn't see Wellingtonia shuffle off. She was still staring after Esmelia.

# 26 Reasons of the Witch

Sam sat on the camp bed in her official competitor's tent and gazed at *Think Yourself Witch*. She was sure now that this was all a terrible mistake. Lilith Dwale hadn't said anything about witches being turned into slithering piles of creepy crawlies before her very eyes and she certainly hadn't mentioned that Esmelia would probably never speak to her again, except maybe to say, "Mmmmm, tasty." She had told *Think Yourself Witch* that she was having second thoughts about becoming Most Superior High and Wicked Witch, but it just sat open on her lap being about as magical as a maths textbook.

With a sigh Sam put it to one side.

There was a rustle at the bottom of the tent. "Pssst," whispered a voice, "Is it safe?"

Sam peered at a head poking under the canvas. "Helza!" she exclaimed, then added, "The potion didn't work. It was a great idea though."

"Forget the potion," whispered Helza Poppin urgently. "Diabolica's gone off somewhere looking like, *totally*, nuts. You can do invisibility spells, right?"

Diabolica was moving through the campsite, being careful to look like she was just out on a shopping trip. She was wearing a hooded cloak and stopped once or twice to look over her shoulder. She lingered a while among tents that had formed a small market selling

magical trinkets, mummy hands and bottles of foul-smelling ointment whose labels advertised "Wart-U-Like: Guaranteed 100% Hairy." Then, when she seemed sure that no one was following, slipped away to a grey tent that stood apart from the others on the very edge of the campsite. The two invisible girls crept forward silently. Sam put her ear to the canvas wall.

"These *children* are driving me crazy," snarled Diabolica's voice. "Years of evil plotting and for what? Do you know how difficult it was to poison Old Biddy Vicious? Have you any idea how many spells I've had to cast to get this far? Not to mention having to be nice to that awful Sniff baggage. She's supposed to be staking the vampire right now and instead she's running around babbling about the wizard's underwear. It's enough to make you sick and we're lucky she's not saying things that would be far worse for us."

The voice that replied Sam had also heard before. Three weeks ago in front of Esmelia's cottage. "Can't you poison them, too, your dramatic gorgeousness?" asked Mandy Snoutley eagerly.

Diabolica ignored her and continued ranting. "I bet it was Igor who swapped my potion ingredients. Betrayed by my own devious little rat of an apprentice.

And this Sam is becoming a nuisance as well. She's far too powerful for an apprentice. It's dangerous…"

Sam stiffened.

"I always say that there's no problem too big that it can't be poisoned away," Mandy interrupted.

Diabolica hesitated. "It's very very tempting, but no. Not now…"

Mandy started to argue and was shushed into silence. "No, not yet." Diabolica told her. "I want their punishment to be slow and painful, so it will have to wait until I'm Most Superior High and Wicked Witch. *Then* I'll take great pleasure in testing out the Bleak Fortress's torture chambers out on both the brats. For now all we need is to get Sam out of the way without any fuss. Esmelia will die quickly after she has finished off the vampire and you, my loathsome hideous Mandy, will make sure that Sam is disqualified. Go and dig something up that will remove her from the competition. You're good at that. Make up a story if you have to. You're good at that too."

"And after?"

"Yes Mandy, after this is over I will mould this ragbag of stupid old women into the most powerful magical force the Earth has ever seen and then the world will be *mine*!" Diabolica laughed. It would be nice to say that it was an evil, menacing, insane laugh, but it was just the normal kind.

"And my reward?"

"What do you want?"

"That time turning potion the girl made. I want some of it. Actually, I want a *lot* of it."

"Dear, vain, ugly, *old* Mandy. You will have it. Now go. Esmelia will be here any moment and you have work to do."

"Yes your evil genius...ss...ness," replied the reporter. There was a shuffle of footsteps and the flap was thrown back. Mandy's broom flew out in a waft of sickly perfume and the reporter disappeared into the sky.

Sam felt Helza's breath as her invisible friend whispered. She turned. Esmelia was striding across the grass towards them with a face as grim as a funeral in the rain.

"I ain't doing it," Esmelia screeched before Diabolica had a chance to say anything. "You can kill your own bloodsucker you primping ninny."

Diabolica sighed. "But Esmelia," she simpered. "It's the only way. You'll never be Most Superior High and Wicked Witch while Cakula lives and besides even vampires sleep sometimes..."

Sam had heard all she needed to. Taking Helza's see-through arm, she pulled her back towards the competitors' tents.

# 27 Ringo Rocks

The sun had gone down. On stage, Esmelia was glaring at Sam, whose stomach sank. Sam felt another pang of regret for having entered the competition. If Esmelia wasn't so angry with her she might have listened to sense. Mentally, Sam cursed Lilith Dwale and then cursed herself. What had she been thinking? Why would she even want to be Most Superior High and Wicked Witch? She missed her comfortable attic and the vicious brambles of Pigsnout Wood – even Esmelia snoring in front of the fire. Looming above, the Bleak Fortress looked cold and draughty and uncomfortable. She didn't want to rule over witches, Sam realized, she just wanted to be a witch, though she wasn't even so sure of that now.

The third round of the trial was Summoning. Diabolica strutted around the stage as usual and Sam found that she couldn't take her eyes off her. She was a murderer. She had killed Old Biddy Vicious and now she was planning to kill Esmelia and then probably her and Helza for good measure. Why did witches have to be so evil, spiteful and *nasty*?

Sam was dimly aware that Esmelia had stepped up to the front of the stage and begun an incantation. Diabolica traced tiny motions in the air and her lips moved slightly as she muttered a spell under her breath. They were cheating again and now Sam knew why. Diabolica wanted Esmelia to win so only the most useless witch (who no one really liked anyway) would stand between her and becoming Most Superior High and Wicked Witch. Well, she told herself, one person didn't hate Esmelia all that much and she was going to stop Diabolica's evil plot, no matter what Mandy Snoutley did to have her disqualified. One thing still confused Sam though. If Diabolica wanted to become Most Superior High and Wicked Witch so much, why hadn't she just entered the trials like everyone else?

Sam's racing mind was brought to an abrupt halt by Esmelia. "Come forth. Come forth. Come blinking forth when I tell you!" the old witch shouted to end her summoning spell. There was a wet slapping sound, a puff of green smoke and foul smell spread around the arena.

"Behold," Esmelia shouted to the audience who were flapping their hands in front of their faces. "I have summoned the demon Boodie-Hodure, Lord of the Sweaty Pit and Master of the Thrice-Worn Sock."

A red-skinned, stinking demon raised an arm and waved to the crowd. As he did so the first three rows of witches caught the full blast of his armpit and leant back in their chairs coughing and spluttering. The demon lowered his arm again quickly, blushing even redder.

"Great," choked Tiffany, who was the closest to the demon and holding her nose. "Can you *un*summon him too?"

With a flick of Esmelia's fingers Boodie-Hodure disappeared. Instead of jeering, for once the crowd gave her a small ripple of applause. It was tricky to summon *any* demon no matter how silly and however much they disliked Esmelia it was an impressive performance.

Next was Callous Meg. Slashing the air with a wand as if she were trying to cut it into ribbons the little witch snarled out a spell. At once, all the lights went out and a terrible blackness gathered on the stage. Sam felt a chill of terror as two red eyes opened at its centre and a terrifying creature stepped out into the arena.

"A banshee, it's a *banshee*," someone whispered.

"The banshee," rasped Callous Meg. "Where will she go? Who will she choose? Be afraid, for she looks only on those who are about to die."

The banshee twisted and turned until its gaze fell upon Cakula von Drakula. With a cruel laugh that made Sam put her hands over her ears, it snapped its wings, landed before the vampire-witch and wailed hideously in her face.

Without her veil, Cakula looked hard and cold. She stood tall, completely uncaring and then a small smile crept across her lips. "Sssorry sstupid creature," she whispered. "Already dead." Then she clicked her fingers. The banshee disappeared with a crack. Cakula swept her own wand out faster than the eye could see and a blast of magic ripped the sky above. An enormous shape on leathery wings dropped through the black tear, its talons stretched out, its mouth open in a shriek of fury.

Sam saw flame at the back of the dragon's throat and then fire leapt out, struck the stage and burned Callous Meg to a smoking cinder.

The vampire-witch swept her wand round again and the dragon vanished as quickly as the banshee. Gazing over the silent audience whose jaws were sagging open, Cakula's smile widened. Moonlight glittered off her fangs. "Oops," she said.

The stage flashed as the lights came back on and Diabolica strolled out whooping. "The dark mistress Cakula von Drakula," she cried, "Isn't she great?"

And Sam understood. Diabolica hadn't entered the competition because she was scared. Scared of that vast, terrifying magic. Petrified of Cakula von Drakula. But if it was *Esmelia* who had to face her then Diabolica could stay safe. And if Esmelia failed to kill Cakula, then who would care that old Stinky Sniff had been eaten by a vampire? Certainly it would be nothing to do with the delightful and still very much alive, host…

Sam suddenly felt very sorry indeed for Esmelia. She glanced at the old witch. She was white as bone and trembling.

"Sam," shouted Diabolica for the third time. "Summon something or you're out."

Sam looked up at her in rage and disgust. She felt the wand twitch in her hand and a temptation to frazzle Diabolica on the spot, but she knew she couldn't do it. She wasn't going to be like other witches. Instead, Sam took a step forward, waved her wand and stammered. Nothing happened.

"I'll have to hurry you dear," smiled Diabolica. Sam felt a fresh wave of hatred for the beautiful, cunning witch wash over her. She took a deep breath and began again, but it was no good. Her mind was a whirl, she couldn't think of anything but how much she hated Diabolica. She couldn't do magic.

There was a familiar
tickling at her neck. Ringo. The little
beetle was calling up magic for her. Sam
could feel it whipping around her body and up
into the wand. She couldn't remember the spell but
she could at least help. Flourishing her wand, Sam pulled
all the magic she could into herself and let the beetle take
control. There was a ripple of purple light and a
summons went out to every corner of Transylvania. For
a moment there was silence and then a hum that grew
louder and louder. Beetles, millions and millions of

beetles, answered Ringo's call. The sky was thick with them. In the light of the great spotlights they formed into a mass that became a living, flying statue of Sam on a broom. It flew around the arena and transformed into the shape of a dragon, twice the size of Cakula's. The crowd gasped as a black flame made of beetles poured from it mouth, then the swarm changed again. This time it took the form of Dr Sulfurus Cowl. And ten million or so beetles slipped away, leaving the wizard standing in his underwear.

Ringo's pincers clicked one last time. In an explosion of black, the beetles swept away toward every horizon, leaving the audience on their feet and stamping their feet as they clapped.

Sam stepped back. She put a hand to her shoulder and stroked Ringo's shiny back. "Ringo," she whispered. "You're a star."

Scowling, Mad Elaine took the stage. It looked like she already knew she was beaten. Nevertheless she wove a complicated spell, during which the crowd held its breath. There was a small pop and the sound of old-fashioned music, the sort that people play on accordions. Under the blazing lights an old man wobbled out onto the stage on an old bicycle. He was wearing a beret, stripy shirt and had a string of onions round his neck. He stopped and looked around at the howling, jeering witches. Sam saw him mouth the words "Sacre bleu," and tug on a small moustache. Then he vanished.

The French witch stomped off stage without waiting for the judges to comment. And sulked for the next six years.

"Just three witches left," yelled Diabolica. "But who's going to win? Will it be the talented apprentice Sam, who came out of nowhere to wow us all? Will it be Esmelia, the witch that everybody loves to hate, but who's taking the competition by storm? Or will Cakula von Drakula taste blood?"

She paused. Smiled.

"Or are there more surprises in store? Find out tomorrow, when you'll meet your new Most Superior High and Wicked Witch!"

# 28 Stake Out

Sam took a deep breath and turned towards Esmelia. Perhaps if she grovelled enough Esmelia might still listen to her. But the old witch had already gone. A hand fell on her shoulder. Sam twisted round and looked into the sparkling green eyes of Diabolica Nightshade. Her heart beat faster. Did the host know her plot had been discovered? Was she going to try and kill her? Sam licked her dry lips, the invisibility spell already forming on them.

"Badness me, you're jumpy," purred the beautiful witch. "I just wanted to ask a teeny favour."

"What?" Sam replied. She could barely keep the fear out of her voice.

Diabolica didn't seem to notice. "That was a wonderful potion you made this morning. I'd love to have a closer look if you have some left."

"I tipped it all away," Sam fibbed. She wasn't going to do Mandy Snoutley any favours.

The hand on her shoulder squeezed tighter. Diabolica smiled. "But I'm sure you could whizz up another batch tonight, couldn't you?"

If she refused, Diabolica might guess something was up, but Sam didn't have time for potions. Her thoughts buzzed for a second, then she said, "Of course, Mistress Nightshade. I'd be happy to."

"That's my girl," Diabolica smiled back.

Esmelia Sniff, wicked witch, sat on the camp bed in her tent staring at the wooden stake in her hand. She wasn't feeling very wicked. In fact, she was feeling like it might be time to retire from the whole witch business. She could just hop on her broom and be away. Maybe take up that nice lady's offer of a place in the village old people's home where the other old folks ate toffees and watched television and – most importantly – didn't summon dragons to burn you to a smoking crisp.

"…So I need your help and if you don't then Esmelia is going to get herself killed."

For once Lilith answered immediately.

*Maybe Esmelia will succeed. She's not quite as useless as you think and most people would say that staking vampires through the heart is a good thing. Haven't you seen the movies?*

"But she's also a witch and even if Esmelia does succeed, Diabolica will kill her later. People – witches – are dying. It has to end."

*You can end it when you're Most Superior High and Wicked Witch.*

Sam started to say something and stopped. Eventually, she said, "I don't *want* to be Most Superior High and Wicked Witch. And besides, Diabolica and Mandy are going to have me disqualified. Why are *you* so keen that I am anyway?"

The book went blank for a moment and then slowly new words appeared: *It's what you were born to be.*

"What? I wasn't born for anything. I'm just an orphan with no family."

*That's not strictly true.*

"I have family? Who? Where? What's a witch child? Tell me. Tell me now."

*Another time. For now you need to win this competition.*

"No. If you don't help me I'm getting on my broom now and flying straight back to the orphanage."

*You have a destiny!*

"I have someone's old hat, a second-hand broom and a large beetle. I don't call that a destiny." There was a clicking sound on her shoulder. "A really wonderful beetle," Sam corrected herself.

*You can defeat Diabolica Nightshade and Cakula too. You haven't even begun to touch your power. It is your destiny! Here's what you should do...*

Sam turned red as Lilith explained her plan. Then she slammed the book. That wouldn't do at all. Sam checked her watch, it was nearly midnight and she needed a plot. She scratched her chin. What was it that Esmelia had said about plotting? Oh yes. Sam turned on the small camp stove provided with her tent. As a pot of water came to a bubbling boil, she stirred it and tried a little cackle. Surprisingly, it really *did* help.

There was a rustle as the flap of Esmelia's tent was pulled aside. She turned her head to see her apprentice standing in the starlight.

Some people, when they are upset, like to take their anger out on someone else. Esmelia was one of those people. Everything was going wrong and as far as she was concerned it was all the lying, slippery little turncoat's fault.

Esmelia drew a deep breath. She didn't need a fire to roast the little toad alive, she'd summon her *own* dragon. Her fingers spread and she spoke the words she'd heard Cakula use earlier. There was a bang and a small hen dropped out of the air with a surprised "bu-kirk." It looked confused for a moment and then started pecking in the dust at Esmelia's feet.

Sam ignored it. "Esmelia," she whispered. "Please listen to me. There's not much time. Diabolica is going to betray you. She's using you to get rid of Cakula von Drakula then she'll kill you and become Most Superior High and Wicked Witch herself."

Esmelia stood, the hen forgotten (though if she had been watching, she would have been slightly cheered to see that it was breathing little puffs of fire). She loomed over her apprentice and sneered "Betrayal is it?" Well, you'd know all about *that* you little worm."

Sam took a step back.

"My own apprentice," Esmelia spat. "What I raised from a baby. Who I taught everything she knows. And how do you repay me you filthy sheep's backside?"

Sam decided it wouldn't be sensible to point out that Esmelia had neither raised her from a baby *nor* taught her everything she knew. "Esmelia, please listen. I...I'm really very sorry. I shouldn't have entered the competition. It's all a terrible mistake and I'll do anything to make it up to you. But we don't have time for that now. Diabolica's going to…"

"No, *you* listen to *me*. I *am* going to be Most Superior High and Wicked Witch and no one is going to stop me. So get lost, but you ain't heard the last of this. I'm planning Sam and Eggs, Honey-glazed Roast Sam and Sam Sandwiches with the leftovers."

"Esmelia, please…"

But Esmelia had her fingers in her ears and was loudly chanting, "LA LA LA LA, NOT LISTENING TO THE SNIVELLING LITTLE MAGGOT."

Sam turned on her heel and left. She hadn't expected it to work, but has had to try anyway. Now Esmelia had left her no choice.

It was the hour before dawn. Esmelia sat down on the bed with sweat dripping down her brow and gripped the stake tightly. Cakula was just a musty old vampire, she thought. One stab with the wooden stake and the bum-headed bloodsucker would be ashes. It would all be over in a second. She just needed a few moments to ready herself. Esmelia closed her eyes and breathed deeply.

Unseen in the corner, the world's first dragon-hen breathed on the canvas of the tent. A fire started.

Ten minutes later, Esmelia stood. "Right!" she shouted out loud. "That's it. I've had enough." She'd been betrayed, people had laughed at her and now her tent was in flames. But, she'd show them. She'd show them all. She was going to be Most Superior High and Wicked Witch. Esmelia stood and with her black cape flying

from her shoulders walked out of the wreckage. Her eyes were burning. And so was her hair.

A corner of Cakula von Dracula's tent twitched aside softly. The warty nose of Esmelia Sniff poked round the flap. It was followed by the warty face of Esmelia Sniff. There was a chittering noise as a flock of bats dropped off the ceiling and whirled around her head. The crone's beady eyes peered into the darkness. She tried a tiny cackle, but it didn't want to come. There was a chair, well, more of a throne really, carved with bats and dragons and other nastier things. On the seat was a ball of black wool with a couple of knitting needles stuck through it. And next to it, on a table, the long shape of Cakula von Drakula's coffin.

Gritting her two teeth to stop them chattering, Esmelia held up her stake and tip-toed across the floor. She reached out a hand. She swung the lid of the coffin back. And screamed. At the exact moment as an incredibly strong, incredibly quick hand reached out from behind.

The hand plucked the stake from Esmelia's grip, whirled her round and clutched her in an embrace of steel. The old witch screamed again as Cakula's teeth glittered above her and then plunged down. She felt two razor sharp points and hot breath at her throat. Esmelia screwed her eyes shut and hoped that having all the blood sucked out of your neck by horrible pointy fangs didn't hurt as much as it sounded like it would.

Cakula leaned back. Her shadow was walking around the walls of the tent rubbing its hands in glee. She chuckled and released the trembling crone who slumped to the floor. "Ssso, Misstress Ssniff," she hissed in a voice that whispered of dark graves and slimy things lurking. "Do I haff your attention?"

Inside the coffin Sam sat up. "If you won't listen to me Esmelia, please listen to Lady von Drakula."

Esmelia's face sagged. Looking between Sam and Cakula von Drakula, she whimpered a little and nodded.

"Vonderful," Cakula said brightly. "Zen zis is vot Sam says ve should do."

# 29 The Wickedest Witch

Storm clouds rumbled, blotting out the sun and lightening flickered across the turrets of the Bleak Fortress. At the front of the stage was a pedestal upon which rested, on a velvet cushion, the Black Wand of Ohh Please Don't Turn Me Into Aaaaarghhh…Ribbett. Sparkles of magic glittered along its length and even from the back of the stage Sam could feel its awesome power.

Three judges and the audience looked on, uneasily, murmuring to each other. Rumours were spreading. Tents had exploded and screams had been heard in the night. A small chicken had been seen breathing fire. What could it all mean?

The lights dimmed. Sad music began to play. Diabolica walked slowly onto the stage. "Ladies of the craft," she began. "There has been foul play. Murder in the night!"

There were 'Oooos" and 'Aaaahs" from the crowd.

"Cakula von Drakula has disappeared. And in her coffin this morning we found this…" Diabolica held up a hand and opened it. Ashes whipped away on the wind.

"And this…" she shouted, holding up a wooden stake.

The audience gasped. Diabolica lowered her head. Her black cloak blew around her. She looked as miserable as it is possible to be. Above thunder rumbled again. Diabolica raised her head, "But we are *witches*," she yelled happily. "We *love* foul play. Murder in the night is what we do *best*."

Music began blaring and lights flashed across the stage, "So let's meet our last two contestants," she laughed. "Sam and Esmelia. A big round of applause please."

The crowd went wild though there were boos when the spotlight settled on Esmelia. She blew a raspberry.

"It was supposed to have been the Transportation Magic this morning," Diabolica continued, "but we're down to the last two so we'll move straight on to the final round, which is traditionally the judges' choice."

She turned to the three judges. "Tiffany, Doris, Sulfurus," she cried. "How is the 173rd trial for the Most Superior High and Wicked Witch going to end?"

The judges went into a huddle. Sam saw Diabolica looking up at the sky. On the panel, there was whispering and a nodding of heads. Tiffany Toadlick stood up. "The final trial will be cursing," she announced. There was a shout of approval. Everyone loved a good cursing.

"Off you go then," said Doris. "Last witch standing wins. Let's have a good fair fight and lots of lovely suffering."

"Yes, let's," Diabolica cut in. There was a tiny speck of black low on the horizon. "Off we go then."

The sky growled. On wings of thunder Mandy Snoutley raced towards the arena.

Esmelia and Sam took opposite sides of the stage. Diabolica shot a look upwards. The speck was slightly bigger now.

Feeling like a gunfighter Sam stared across the stage into Esmelia's eyes. Deep within them, there was a little flicker of glee. Sam hoped the old witch remembered the plan. Despite the promises she'd made last night she still looked very much like a nasty old crone out for revenge. Sam found herself nervously wondering: could you trust a witch?

Slowly, Esmelia reached into a pocket and pulled out a little wax doll. Cursing was the area of magic she'd always been best at. There was nothing glittery or silly about a good, old-fashioned curse. "Thepainofahundredpins," she barked and jabbed at the doll. Sam felt a searing pain in her leg and clutched it with a squeal.

There was a burst of applause.

"Oww," Sam squealed. "That *really* hurt." It wasn't *supposed* to have hurt. Well, not that much.

"Teach you to go around betraying innocent old witches, eh?" leered Esmelia. She flicked her doll.

What felt like a large boot kicked Sam up the bottom. With another howl, she jumped three foot in the air. Esmelia was cackling now. Well, Sam thought, if the crone wanted to be like that, she could too. She clutched her wand. You didn't need wax dolls. Esmelia was just showing off. It was easy enough to curse without them. Particularly when you had power like she did.

"…and set fire to your warts," she yelled flicking her wand at Esmelia.

"Ouch, ouch, ouch," said Esmelia, smiling the smile of someone who would never get smiling right. Her warts were *not* on fire.

Drat, thought Sam, she had forgotten. Still, she had to try, just for the look of it. "This is for giving rubbish broom-riding lessons," she shouted at the old witch. "Turn the marrow of your bones to ice and fill your insides full of lice!" She turned the wand on Esmelia once more and the crone was surrounding by a glowing haze of powerful magic.

"Rubbish," snorted Esmelia. "Let's see you do another spell when you can't breathe." She gripped the

wax doll in her fist and Sam felt the air squeezed out of her. She gasped, her eyes bulging and looked across to see Esmelia's bony fingers curling harder and harder. Wax was oozing between them…

Thunder rolled once more. The speck was now a witch, hunched over a broom, hurtling towards the stage. Sam no longer cared. She couldn't breathe. It felt like a huge snake was coiled around her. All the threats and put-downs stupid old Esmelia had thrown at her over the last three weeks welled up inside and tears came to her eyes. Why had she wanted to be a witch so much? Well, it didn't matter any more. It looked like Esmelia was going to crush her.

"Stop!" cried Diabolica into her microphone. Above, Mandy Snoutley circled, looking pleased with herself. "I believe *The Cackler* has something to say."

Every witch in the audience booed. The cursing had just been getting going. Slowly, Sam felt the grip on her lessen. She could breathe again. Rubbing her chest, she scowled at Esmelia, who winked back. The old witch stepped across the stage to stand next to her apprentice. She put a hand on Sam's shoulder. "I wouldn't really have killed you," Esmelia whispered, then added to herself, "not when it'd waste all them delicious dinners."

Mandy dropped to the stage waving a piece of

paper. "Gorgeous young lovely, Mandy Snoutley from *The Cackler*," she shouted. "This trial is null and void. One of Sam's recommendations can't be counted!"

A gasp of shock rang around the arena. This was shaping up even better than the cursing.

"Lilith Dwale had her licence taken away." Mandy yelled in excitement. "She wasn't a witch so she can't recommend anyone. I have here a top secret paper saying that she was discharged from the craft for having a baby!"

Sam gasped.

Diabolica stepped to the front of the stage and lifted the Black Wand of Ohh Please Don't Turn Me Into Aaaaarghhh…Ribbett. She twitched it. Glints of power fell from the end. Diabolica lifted it so every witch in the audience could see. Above her, lightening flashed and a mist curled around her feet.

"Then I hereby pronounced Esmelia Sniff 173rd Most Superior High and Wicked Witch," Diabolica yelled.

Esmelia grinned hungrily. Sam felt bony fingers digging into her shoulder. The audience erupted into boos.

"But wait…" Diabolica began. She was staring around at the audience with a look of disbelief on her face. "That old *hag*? Our *leader*? She couldn't win a toenail in a cut-your-own-toenails competition. Surely we can't allow her to become Most Superior High and Wicked Witch, can we?"

"Oi! There ain't nothing wrong with hags…" began Really-Very-Beautiful-Now Doris.

Her voice was drowned by the audience of witches. As one they cried, "Noooo!"

"You cheating earwig. That's my wand you're waving about," sneered Esmelia stepping forward. "Give it me."

Diabolica ignored her, she turned to the audience again, a sea of mist around her ankles. "Do you want your leader to be a maggot-brained ditch-witch who'll have you all burning at the stake?" she bellowed. "Or do you want a *real* witch? A witch who will lead you to *glory*? A witch who will make you powerful beyond your wildest dreams?"

"A real witch! A real witch!" chanted the crowd.

"Then I grant your wish," yelled Diabolica. She spun and pointed the Black Wand of Ohh Please Don't Turn Me Into Aaaaarghhh…Ribbett. A blaze of black fire poured from its tip and wrapped itself around Esmelia. She struggled and screamed. A touch too dramatically Sam thought, though no one else seemed to notice.

It should have killed her, but magic doesn't work

on those who have drunk deeply of Helza Poppin's Immune To Magic potion. Even the vast power of the Black Wand of Please Don't Turn Me Into… Aaaargh Ribbett, could not touch Esmelia now. With one last "Oh poor me, I'm dying," she dropped to the floor. She looked dead, but didn't need to act much. Having her tent burned down and nearly being bitten by a vampire had left her looking a bit peaky.

Diabolica raised her arms. Her smile widened. Now nothing could stop her.

Sam stepped forward. She too was smiling grimly. It was her turn now. "Wicked Witching time, Ringo," she whispered and felt the beetle begin calling up magic. She added hers to it. Lilith had said that she hadn't begun to touch her power and now Sam started to believe her. She could feel a huge well of it inside her, deeper than the seas and connected to the Earth and everything on it. An unimaginable well of magic. And it was hers for the taking. It fizzed around her. The air sparkled and she floated above the stage, surrounded by flashing colour.

"You? Most Superior High and Wicked Witch?" Sam jeered. "You killed Old Biddy Vicious. You're a coward, a liar, a thief and a murderer. And worse than that you're a primping ninny and a terrible witch."

Diabolica's eyes fixed on Sam as the apprentice slowly raised her wand. For a second fear flashed in them. Sam sent a fury of boiling power cascading across the stage.

It was flicked harmlessly into the air by the Black Wand of Ohh Please Don't Turn Me Into Aaaaarghhh…Ribbett. Diabolica gave a pretty laugh and said, "Really dear, is that the best you can do?"

For a tiny moment Sam looked into her green eyes and felt something like jealousy. To have that much magic, it was almost worth… She glanced at Esmelia, looking dead on the stage. There was still time to switch to Lilith's plan. With the Black Wand of Ohh Please Don't Turn Me Into Aaaaarghhh…Ribbett and her own magic she could be the most powerful witch ever. Why, if she wanted to she could rule the world. The thought lasted less than a second. She wouldn't become like Diabolica. No, Sam told herself. Her life wasn't going to be like that. The lights around her faded and she dropped to the ground.

"Well, well," Diabolica drawled, never taking her eyes off Sam. Mist was rising behind her. "Perhaps, Tiffany, before I put an end to this once and for all we could give Sam a lesson in what it means to be a witch. Why don't you tell us what the rulebook says about the only remaining contestant in the competition being killed by a power-crazed evil sorceress who has been plotting for years?"

Tiffany leafed through the enormous book, her eyes flickering across to where Diabolica stood in front of a thickening column of mist.

"Umm," Tiffany said finally. "It says here that if the only remaining witch in the competition is killed by a power-crazed evil sorceress who has been plotting for years… Well, the Most Superior High and Wicked Witch is whoever is left holding the Black Wand of Ohh Please Don't Turn Me Into Aaaaarghhh…Ribbett. But…"

"Oh my word, that would be me!" Still staring at Sam, Diabolica giggled. And now, when she finally won, it turned into a proper mad, menacing laugh, "Ah ha ha HA…" she began and whipped the wand around her head. Above the clouds swirled into a whirlwind. Strange lights flashed. Diabolica was preparing to do some *serious* magic and Sam was going to be on the receiving end. "AH HA HA," she continued.

Her eyes were still fixed on Sam's. If she had looked behind her she would have noticed the column of mist turn into the figure of a tall woman with a terrible hairstyle. She might have seen long white fingers tipped with razor-sharp nails reach out…

"No, you haff it all wrong," said Cakula von

Drakula, plucking the wand out of Diabolica's hand. "It's not 'Ah ha ha ha.' It's *MWAH* ha ha HA HA *HA*!"

"No," replied Sam at last, with satisfaction in her voice. "*That's* the best I can do." She bowed to the vampire-witch who had arrived bang on time.

"Sank you Sam." Cakula returned the bow and turned to face a murderous looking Diabolica. "Ssoo," Cakula hissed. "Tricked by a pointy stick and a handful off ashes in a coffin. You are a fool Mistress Not-so-Deadly Nightshade. A fool not fit to lead witches… And Biddy Vicious was a friend off mine.'"

The vampire-witch towered over Diabolica, her face lined with cruelty, her eyes burning red and her fangs white and sharp. Cakula looked terrifying. She raised the Black Wand of Ohh Please Don't Turn Me Into Aaaaarghhh…Ribbett.

"Oh drat!" swore Diabolica. "Mandy!"

The reporter's broom swept across the stage and Diabolica jumped on. As the two witches tore into the sky Cakula threw her head back and laughed, properly, as a mad laugh was supposed to be laughed. Thunder boomed in answer and lightening poured into the most powerful wand in the world. Still laughing, Cakula pointed it at the fleeing broom.

"No," shouted Sam, grabbing Cakula's iron arm.

"No more killing. Let her go."

Slowly, the vampire lowered the wand. "Very vell," she murmured. "But no more favours."

Esmelia climbed to her feet, looking crabby. She had been enjoying the chance for a quick nap and still hadn't had breakfast. "You ain't the only witch left you know," she interrupted grumpily. "There's still two of us in this competition."

Cakula von Dakula turned to her. "You vould fight *me*?" she asked. "In a battle off curses?"

"Oh," Esmelia replied. She could feel Helza's potion wearing off. "I forgot about that bit. No, no. Not to worry. As you were – laughing and lightning and all that."

As one, every witch in the audience got to her feet and cheered. They had a new Most Superior High and Wicked Witch. Plus, it had been excellent entertainment. Sam clapped politely and went to stand next to Esmelia as a good apprentice should. She felt the old witch squeeze her arm, as if checking to see how much meat there was on it. Which is –of course – exactly what she was doing.

Miles away, Diabolica still had the microphone. She raised it to her lips and her voice echoed around the arena one last time. "Fools! Bony crones and muttering hags, you think you can stop me?" she shrieked. "It's not over yet! I'm a power-crazed evil sorceress. *Nothing* can stop me! *Mwah* ha ha HA *HA!*"

Diabolica's insane laughter gurgled into a scream. Just behind the broom a dragon dropped out of thin air. Its great leathery wings flapped once. Twice. With a flaming roar it set off after the escaping witches.

"Don't vorry," said Cakula, turning to Sam and lowering her new wand, "It von't kill many of them!"

Sam watched the broom carrying two panic-stricken witches disappear over the horizon with the dragon in close pursuit. There was something about Diabolica, she thought... And then her attention was distracted. A pirate had jumped on stage and was waving a string bag at everyone "Ah harrr me hearties," he cried. "Here's bananas for all o' ye."

Tiffany took a bow.

# Epilogue

Back in the cottage, Esmelia reached down her best and biggest roasting tin and bent over to build up the fire in the stove, using the bellows to get it hotter. As she did so Sam strolled into the kitchen, dressed in jeans and reading *The Cackler* with a brightly polished Ringo perched on her shoulder. She paused for a second without taking her eyes off the page and tipped the old witch into the oven with her toe, then pushed the door closed with a clang. Sam rolled her eyes. Really, she thought, it was too easy. Esmelia should try reading some fairy tales sometime.

She looked down at the green warty face pressed against the glass, shouting curses that Sam couldn't hear and decided that Esmelia could sweat for a few minutes. It would be nice to have some peace and quiet and catch up on her reading. It wasn't *really* nasty, she told herself. The oven wasn't very hot yet and she wouldn't let Esmelia *actually* cook. For a start she would taste horrid. And besides, that business with the wax doll had really hurt.

Sam returned her attention to newspaper. Mandy

Snoutley had been sacked, she noticed and true to her word Cakula von Drakula had used her power as Most Superior High and Wicked Witch to release Helza Poppin from her apprenticeship to Diabolica Nightshade. Sam sighed and put the paper aside. She pulled a book towards her across the table and tapped the cover of *Think Yourself Witch* for the twentieth time. "I know you're in there Lilith Dwale," she said. "Is there something you want to tell me?"

She opened the book and at last writing began squirming across the page.

*If you'd followed MY plan you could still've won it*, she read. *And I ain't your mother if that's what you're thinking.*

A tear trickled down Sam's face. As she watched, the writing began to tangle into new shapes. Now it spelled, *But I am your grandmother.*

Sam cried some more and half an hour later remembered to let Esmelia out of the oven. But only after she promised to become a vegetarian.

A little later Sam did the washing up.

Outside a spooky mansion was a sign that said, "Help wanted: must be hunchback called Igor with one eye bigger than the other."

Deep within, Deadly Nightshade tossed a jar of clear liquid to her faithful servant. "Oh," she said, "I nearly forgot. This is for you."

With a moan of pleasure, Mandy Snoutly scrabbled the lid off and drank the potion. At once a white light surrounded her and her face began to melt. Mandy screamed with joy. At last she was going to be young and beautiful again. The light grew more intense and then blinked out. Where Mandy had been sitting was a gigantically ugly woman of roughly 238. Her face was covered with hairy warts and spots and wrinkles so deep that folds of skin were almost dragging along the floor. Her corsets snapped and great rolls of flab burst out of her tiny dress. She was completely bald.

"Aaarrrrrgh," shrieked Mandy Snoutley. "AaaaaaRRGGGGGH!!!!"

Helza Poppin really was *extremely* good at potions.